SPECIAL MESSAGE TO READERS

THE ULVERSCROFT FOUNDATION
(registered UK charity number 264873)

was established in 1972 to provide funds for research, diagnosis and treatment of eye diseases. Examples of major projects funded by the Ulverscroft Foundation are:-

- The Children's Eye Unit at Moorfields Eye Hospital, London
- The Ulverscroft Children's Eye Unit at Great Ormond Street Hospital for Sick Children
- Funding research into eye diseases and treatment at the Department of Ophthalmology, University of Leicester
- The Ulverscroft Vision Research Group, Institute of Child Health
- Twin operating theatres at the Western Ophthalmic Hospital, London
- The Chair of Ophthalmology at the Royal Australian College of Ophthalmologists

You can help further the work of the Foundation by making a donation or leaving a legacy. Every contribution is gratefully received. If you would like to help support the Foundation or require further information, please contact:

THE ULVERSCROFT FOUNDATION
The Green, Bradgate Road, Anstey
Leicester LE7 7FU, England
Tel: (0116) 236 4325

website: www.foundation.ulverscroft.com

WHISPERS ON THE PLAINS

Widowed wheat farmer Dusty Nash, of Sunday Plains pastoral station, is captivated by the spirited redhead who arrives in the district. Irish teacher Meghan Dorney has left her floundering engagement for a six-month posting to the outback of Western Australia. Thrown together in the small, isolated community, each resists their budding attraction to resolve personal issues and tragedy. But when Dusty learns the truth about the newcomer, can he forgive enough to love?

NOELENE JENKINSON

WHISPERS ON THE PLAINS

Complete and Unabridged

LINFORD
Leicester

First published in Great Britain in 2014

First Linford Edition
published 2015

A catalogue record for this book is available
from the British Library.

ISBN 978–1–4448–2584–8

Published by
F. A. Thorpe (Publishing)
Anstey, Leicestershire

Set by Words & Graphics Ltd.
Anstey, Leicestershire
Printed and bound in Great Britain by
T. J. International Ltd., Padstow, Cornwall

This book is printed on acid-free paper

1

'I tell you, Claire, outback Western Australia couldn't be any flatter. There's nothing but red dirt and scruffy-looking grass.'

'You woke me all the way over here in Ireland to tell me that?'

Meghan smiled at her friend's grumpy words. 'Stranded out here in the middle of nowhere, it hits you how different this country is from Ireland and its forty shades of green.'

'Is the rescue vehicle coming yet?'

Meghan shaded her eyes and scanned in either direction along the deserted road. 'Not yet. They said I'm closer to Mallawa now than the coast so they're sending someone out from town.'

'Well, with a flat tyre, you'd better hope it's a handy fella.'

'I just hope he makes it before dark.' She eyed the lowering sun. 'After flying for twenty hours from Dublin to Perth then jumping on an afternoon flight up to Geraldton and driving for hours in the outback, I'm jiggered.'

'Do you want me to stay on the line?'

'No. I'd best save my phone battery in case of another emergency.'

'This call will be costing you a fortune.'

Meghan was about to end the call when she added eagerly, 'A vehicle's coming from the direction of town.'

'Probably be your fella then.'

'To be honest, Claire, with no traffic, I hope it's any man who can help me from being stuck out here all night.'

'Now now, Meggie,' her friend chided, 'Don't go fancying any big strong outback men. Remember poor old pining Dermot back here.'

Meghan frowned in frustration at the mention of her fiancé. 'I'm trying not to. That's why I came out here in the first place, remember?'

'He's not that bad,' she defended. 'He loves you to bits.'

Meghan paused. 'He loves his job

more, Claire, and you know it. He's powerful ambitious.'

'You'll hurt him,' she warned.

'He hardly knows I exist anymore. Maybe we're not meant to be together.'

'You're letting on!' Claire sounded surprised. 'You adore each other.'

True, she had. Once. Except Meghan wasn't so sure she held the same feelings for him these days. When had that changed?

Focusing on the new arrival pulling up across the road, Meghan stifled a gasp of admiration. A tall man unwound himself from the vehicle, slammed the door of his four-wheel drive in desperate need of a wash, and started walking toward her. Wearing dusty jeans, a big and equally dusty hat and black T-shirt, this was some gorgeous saviour. But didn't he feel the cold in short sleeves? She shivered. No matter. If this was a random sample of Australian men, things were looking up.

'I've just seen a god,' she whispered to Claire as the muscled long legs brought the man closer.

'Oh Meggie honey, you've probably got heat stroke.' Claire sounded concerned.

'Eejit. It's almost dark. Besides, it's the middle of winter over here yet it only feels as chilly as a soggy summer in Ireland. Slán.' She swiftly tapped her phone and ended the call.

With a quick side glance to the flat back right-hand tyre, the athletic man gaped at her until she stopped talking. 'You the new teacher?'

She stuffed her mobile in her padded vest pocket, shrugged it closer around her against the crisp late afternoon air and nodded. 'Meghan Dorney.'

His big sun-browned hand was rough to the touch when she shook it. 'Dusty Nash. I'm on the welcoming committee.'

Meghan stopped herself from spluttering with laughter. He sure was. Dusty. Covered in the red stuff from hat to boots. He eyeballed her bluntly up and down.

To cover her embarrassment at being so closely inspected, she said, 'Grateful my phone worked out here.'

'People were getting worried. They were expecting you hours ago.'

'My plane was late and I didn't plan this.' She glanced at the deflated tyre.

'Out here, you should know how to change one yourself.' She blinked at his bluntness. 'Pop the boot so I can get started and you can follow me into town.'

She did as he instructed and he was soon setting up the jack, undoing wheel nuts and rolling the flat tyre aside before replacing it with the spare. Meghan leant against the car with her arms folded, watching her brawny rescuer make short work of his job. If he wasn't so grumpy, she might find herself admiring the man. She banished thoughts of Dermot.

Her tyre man wasn't big on conversation so she gazed around the countryside. She had already marvelled at its vastness and huge distances in the last few hours of lonely driving without seeing another vehicle. The Australian outback was big and flat with nothing between you and the horizon except for a few distant trees. She hadn't sighted a kangaroo yet and she was looking forward to that. The land paraded a tinge of green now but she had been warned about the hot summers with no rain. She wondered what she'd make of it all in six months' time when her work visa expired and she returned to Ireland for Christmas.

Dusty rose to his feet, stowed the flat tyre in the boot and closed it again. 'So how much further's town then?' she asked him.

'Fifteen minutes.' He pulled an oily rag from his back pocket and wiped his hands.

'It's powerful country out here.' She swept a glance around it again. 'It's about as far removed as you can get from anything or anyone. I can travel across most of Ireland in the same amount of time its taken to get out to

Mallawa.' She grinned.

His tanned face promised a smile but only his eyes crinkled up at the corners. Might have a sense of humour buried deep, but she judged this man didn't easily let it out. 'There are places more remote than this. Some folk have to drive all day to reach a neighbour.'

'You're letting on,' she scoffed.

He shrugged, sure of himself and unconcerned. 'It's a fact.' He moved away. 'We're ready to roll. Just follow me and the road, but you'll hardly get lost.'

★   ★   ★

As Dusty walked away and folded himself back into his vehicle, he felt a need to feast another look at this newcomer. He never paid attention to females these days but he liked her lilting accent and up-front manner; those big green eyes that stared directly at you. It suggested confidence and strength.

Her rusty long hair spilled around her face and shoulders in wild waves. She'd have to tie that lot back in summer and cover her pale skin and freckles with a slather of sunscreen when summer hit. A striking woman, if a man was interested. Looked a mite fragile for the outback but seemed cheerful enough. A sense of male protection kicked into play and he determined to watch out for her as he gunned the motor and headed back into town. He glanced in his rear-view mirror to check her car was following. He figured it was best to take her straight to the house they'd leased for her. Give her a chance to unload and settle in for an hour or two before the welcome barbeque the committee had arranged.

* * *

Meghan felt safe trailing Dusty's vehicle. This outback adventure promised to be exciting. Until you were stuck out in the middle of it alone without any help. Dermot would have fussed and treated her like a piece of porcelain. Dusty Nash expected her to cope, but he would be around in a crisis.

It was a pleasant change from being stifled by Dermot. Growing up together, she'd accepted his habits. Now they grated on her nerves. With his rising success in business, he'd become bossy and controlling. Meghan had considered the change a product of his drive and ambition but since their engagement, he treated her like just another piece of the property portfolio he was accumulating. Flinging out commands and expecting her to succeed, too.

It troubled her that their future marriage wouldn't be a partnership, so her cold feet had rallied her to raise the courage to escape for a while. Test the waters of life without him, think about her fading love and reassess it from a distance. He had been furious when she told him her plans. His hurt male pride exploded because she had dared make a decision without him. But if they were to survive as a couple, he'd best get used to it, because Meghan Dorney was no man's doormat.

The long flight from Ireland to Australia had allowed her to contemplate Dermot's heavy-handed approach to their union. No date was set, but he was pushing for a summer wedding until she had told him she'd be teaching in outback Australia for six months under a skilled regional response programme. She'd stood her ground, listened to his warnings, and had finally walked away, aching with hurt and disappointment at his inflexibility and arrogance.

Her mind was so buried in thought she was forced to suddenly brake when the red tail-lights of Dusty's vehicle ahead loomed closer and his right blinker flashed. They slowed at a T-intersection and turned into town. Meghan was awed by its broad casual main road, so sprawling compared to the neat villages of Ireland, where houses hugged the streets. Dusty's arm was casually draped over his open window and he waved to every person they passed.

They wheeled into a side street, pulled into the driveway of a timber home with an iron roof, and parked under a carport. So this was to be home for the next six months. She peered at it excitedly. Dusty waited, jiggling what looked like her house keys, so she got out and joined him.

'It's basic, but it's been recently renovated by working bees of locals, so we hope you find it comfortable.'

'I'm sure it will be grand.' She eyed it with positive curiosity and smiled, following him through a side gate onto a back porch. He unlocked the door and stepped aside. 'Thank you,' she murmured, impressed by this small gentlemanly gesture from such a macho individual.

They wandered into a neat kitchen with a small round dining table at one end, as well as stone patterned linoleum and plenty of pale green cupboards for storage. It looked a mite dated, nothing fancy for sure, but homely. She had no unrealistic expectations of life out here in a remote community, but everything appeared clean and fresh. Inside and out, men's and women's hands had been busy.

'The ladies on the welcoming committee have been in already.' He followed her gaze to the small vase of strange flowers on the table.

'What are these?' She gently fingered the red curly tendrils of the blooms in the arrangement.

'Grevillea. Native spider flowers.'

'They're gorgeous. I'm not much of a gardener, I'm afraid. I'm more at home in a kitchen.' Her eye was caught by her favourite appliance in any house. 'That's some cooker.' Her excitement was tempered by his frown. Had she said something wrong?

'Oh, you mean the stove.'

She grinned. 'Is that what you call it here?' She predicted some future misunderstandings with language differences.

He strode over to the refrigerator and opened the door. 'The ladies have stocked this for you, and the pantry.' He glanced toward the full-length cupboard with double doors. 'But we have a good IGA here in town if you need anything.'

'Is that some kind of store?'

'Our local grocer.'

'Right. Grand.'

He seemed uncomfortable indoors, yet out on the deserted country road had been completely at ease. He was avoiding her gaze but gave her a quick glance as he said, 'I'll give you the rest of the guided tour.' He led her into the adjoining living area complete with a long sofa and chairs set around an unlit open fireplace. Small logs of wood were piled high in a basket on the hearth and a television stood across a far corner.

'This is lovely,' she said warmly and caught his cautious gaze. He seemed to be watching for her reactions as though expecting her to turn and run back to Perth and catch the first flight home. 'I'm guessing the bedroom and bath are through there?' She nodded at the open double doors that led into a hallway and headed toward them ahead of him to prompt proceedings along a little. She didn't want to appear rude or unappreciative, but she'd been travelling nonstop for more than a day and was exhausted, longing to unpack and take a bath.

'It's nothing fancy,' he said almost apologetically.

'On the contrary, it looks to have everything I could possibly need and I'm grateful.'

His raised eyebrows, letting her know he was surprised by her comment. Meghan felt irritated that he considered her such a lightweight who would apply for a job then travel halfway around the world without doing some decent research about what was at the other end of her destination. In recent months since getting the post, part of which covered the Irish summer holidays anyway, she had relentlessly surfed the internet and grabbed every book on Australia and especially the outback that she could lay her hands on in the local library and bookshops in town and Dublin.

'I'll get your bags from the car so you can unpack. The locals have organised a welcome barbeque later, so you'll get to meet some of them as well as your fellow teachers and families.' He made her heavy suitcase seem as light as a small briefcase the way he hauled it inside and set it down on her bed. 'Barbie's at seven, so I'll swing by just before and pick you up.'

'Oh, there's no need, surely.' Meghan protested. 'I have a car — '

'I'm the chairman of the committee. It's my job,' he said bluntly.

Meghan took a mental step back at his frank response, realising she was considered an obligation. So far, she had gained the impression that the townsfolk were nothing but friendly and hospitable, so it was a jolt of reality to receive such a candid retort.

'Grand. I'll see you around seven then.'

'Don't forget to take that spare tyre into the garage to be fixed.'

Meghan nodded, forcing a smile, and jammed her hands into her back pockets trying to appear unconcerned about his harsh parting shot.

When he was gone, Meghan let out a long, slow sigh and wandered slowly back through the house, opening and closing cupboards in the kitchen, wardrobes in the bedroom. The house was well supplied. Towels and toiletries were laid out in the bathroom with another small glass vase of the spidery red flowers she'd seen in the kitchen. She smiled softly. It meant something to sense neighbourly touches way out here in a place far stranger than anything she had ever seen before. Even on all the backpacking she'd done with Claire over the years every chance she could get.

To help ward off her weariness, she made herself a strong coffee to drink while she unpacked. For now in the cooler months she'd be wearing mostly jeans and T-shirts, and her smarter teaching clothes during the week, but she'd allowed for the warmer weather that was sure to come by tossing in some pairs of denim and cargo shorts with tank tops plus a few pretty dresses for good measure.

She'd thrown open a couple of windows to let the light early-evening breezes freshen up the house. In the quiet of being alone and in a residential street of an outback town with little traffic, her ears pricked at any sound. When she heard a car engine outside rumble to a stop, she panicked for a moment and checked the fancy designer gold watch Dermot had given her for her last birthday.

She feared it was Dusty Nash returning already until a resounding confident knocking echoed loudly from the back door through the house and a female voice called out, 'Hello there.'

Someone had let themselves into her kitchen. Meghan strode down the hallway to greet her as the homely and smiling elderly woman placed a covered earthenware dish on the table. 'Miss Dorney, is it?'

'Meghan, please.' She smiled warmly.

'Noreen Williams.' Her visitor beamed.

'And what do you have there, then?' She nodded toward what was clearly some heavenly-smelling food.

'Just a lamb casserole that should do you for a meal or two. Probably not a lot different to an Irish stew,' she chuckled. 'Put it in the refrigerator before you come to the barbeque and don't worry about the dish. I can collect it anytime or you can drop it off at the school. I help with reading in the library.'

'That's right generous of you.'

'Well,' she said, crinkling up her nose and grinning, 'until you find your way about it will all be a bit strange. You can safely wander anywhere in town to get your bearings. I can guarantee word has spread and everyone will know you. If not by your lovely Irish accent then certainly by that red hair,' she chuckled.

Humbly flattered, Meghan said, 'Thank you. I guess they will.'

'Now I know you won't have had time to hardly catch your breath, and I hear you had a spot of car trouble out the road, but if there's anything you need or if you have any questions, just ask anyone. You'll find a list of phone numbers on the inside of the pantry door. Ring one of them and they'll put you right. Now,' she rattled straight on, 'some of the women are on a roster to bring you a meal once a week for a while. That way it's a chance for a friendly chat if you need to talk to someone, and it'll help you get to know us better.'

'Sounds grand.'

'Well, I'll be off then.' Noreen bustled to the door. 'Put that casserole in the fridge and I'll see you later at the barbeque. It won't be late. It's been a long day travelling for you and everyone will have kids to get to bed. No school tomorrow, being a Sunday, so that should give you a day to catch up on sleep and feel your way. And some of the lads to recover if they have a few too many tonight.' She chuckled again and disappeared.

2

Finally, peace descended for Meghan. No more visitors. She finished her coffee and unpacking then, despite the strong possibility of falling asleep, took a good long soak in the bath. When her eyelids grew heavy and the water cooled, she forced herself out and wondered how dressy a local barbeque might be. She guessed her Aran jumper and denims would be adequate.

She towelled the damp ends of her hair and gave it a brisk brush to sort out the tangles. She was just attempting to cover up her freckles with a light dusting of powder when she heard another vehicle outside. Sliding her feet into a pair of comfortable low heels, she checked her watch and the kitchen clock to confirm it was almost seven. Must be Dusty returning on time. She was accustomed to reliability gained from serving in her parents' pub and keeping a classroom of children in line.

Meghan was feeling reserved about socialising with Dusty at a casual function. He seemed a mite stiff and uncomfortable out on the road and back here in the house, but she judged him an honest and genuine sort of fella. Not pushy like Dermot. She gave herself a mental slap. She must stop criticising poor Dermot when he didn't have a chance to defend himself. But held up and compared against other men, he rarely measured up favourably anymore these days. He was certainly no longer the boy she grew up with.

Dusty Nash might have a wife or girlfriend in the wings but, regardless, she hoped they could break down whatever the barrier was between them and at least become friends. Might be that he was just the strong, silent type.

When he knocked, she gathered up a light coat, wrapped a scarf around her bag handles in case the night grew nippy later, and greeted him with a smile. She was blown away by the change. His dusty everyday working clothes were gone, replaced by clean fitted jeans and a black corded jacket zipped halfway up over a striped shirt. His light brown wavy hair now rippled free of his big hat.

'Hi,' he said softly, gaping, then cleared his throat and asked, 'Feeling better?'

She nodded, not flattering herself that his stare was any kind of interest. 'It was a grand long bath that did it,' she chuckled as she moved past him toward his vehicle. He sprinted up behind her and opened her door. She sent him a warm smile, surprised and amused. 'Thank you.'

A mere two-minute drive brought them to a community hall at a recreation oval already buzzing with lights and people. Children were running about and knots of people stood chatting with a drink. 'We could have walked,' Meghan laughed. 'Quite a turnout.'

Dusty eyed her carefully. 'The town appreciated your application. It's always challenging to persuade people to come and live and work in the outback. Even on temporary work visas.'

'I'd have thought it would be considered an exciting experience.'

He shrugged. 'Maybe to someone from Ireland.'

Meghan soon grew accustomed to loads of interested glances turned in their direction as she walked with Dusty toward the crowds. The smell of cooking meat whipped up her appetite, making her groan, for she'd only picked at generic airline food all day.

She was immediately flung into a constant round of introductions and new faces and shook so many hands she was starting to feel like the Queen. Bit different to home where she was always just Miss Dorney to the children or Meggie behind the bar. It was all such fun, and she was the centre of attention. She caught Dusty watching her occasionally and once or twice he ambled over to enquire that all was well.

And from the dark-skinned faces among the crowd, she realised there was a percentage of Aboriginal population here as well. Apart from town identities like the shire councillor and the headmistress of Mallawa Independent School where she would teach, there were also football players, farmers' sons and local tradesmen hovering around or sending glances in her direction.

When first offered a drink by one of many male admirers, she asked for a beer. Upon its arrival, she looked at it twice before commenting, 'This is a pale cousin to the black stuff I'm accustomed to in Ireland.'

'Guinness is awful stuff,' one handsome young man said with a wink.

She smiled, accepting the banter with ease. 'I disagree,' she argued. 'My father owns a pub in Rathdrum. I've been pulling my share of beers since I was sixteen and it's the most popular drink in the house.'

She realised Dusty had reappeared at

her side when he said quietly, 'A young woman of many talents,' for once letting those warm hazelnut eyes linger over her face.

'Grub's up,' one of the men manning the barbeque yelled out.

A general crush of people made for the grill to grab a paper plate and cutlery to receive their meat before heading for the long tables draped with white cloths sagging beneath mountains of food.

'Looks like the ladies have catered for an army again,' Dusty said wryly at her elbow.

Meghan was amazed at the variety: salads, breads, cheesecakes, a scrumptious-looking meringue with whipped cream and strawberries. 'A pavlova,' Noreen Williams explained from across the table as she piled salads onto her plate along with a lamb chop and a banger. 'It's just whipped egg whites and sugar slow-baked until it's crispy on the outside and marsh-mallow in the middle.'

Always fascinated by new foods and dishes, Meghan moaned with pleasure at the tempting sound and contemplated whether to skip the first course and go straight to the afters. 'I'm into baking,' she admitted. 'Could I have the recipe, do you think, then? I've that lovely big cooker at my place.'

'I'll write it out for you soon as I find a scrap of paper and a pen. Remind me before I leave.'

'That'd be grand, thanks.'

Looking around, she made her way to snatch a spare seat on a hay bale since most other chairs or benches around the walls were already occupied. She chatted easily within a circle of young folk and a few sets of parents, plus one or two of her fellow teachers who had already introduced themselves and settled nearby.

Meghan soon found the motherly Noreen by her side again. 'Don't mind if I share a hay bale, do you?' Meghan shook her head and shuffled further along. 'My Ted's on his shift rota out at the Koolanooka mine so he won't be home for another week.'

'What do they mine?'

'Iron ore. They've just reopened it in recent years. They export it out through Geraldton to China.'

'How far away is it?'

'About twenty kilometres east of town. It's an open pit and there are two more the better part of an hour further east at Blue Hills.'

'Do many locals work out there?'

'Those that want the work for sure.'

'Do you have family?'

Noreen nodded. 'A couple of sons. They both work out at the mine driving those giant dump trucks.'

'Tough work and conditions, I imagine.'

'Good salary though. A man can earn six figures a year.' Meghan raised her eyebrows at the amazing news. 'Lucrative for a young man starting out in life. The company has plans to expand even more further inland beyond Meekatharra.'

Meghan had no idea where that could possibly be and decided not to ask since her head was already buzzing with information and names and strange new foods. She finished her salads and was just contemplating wandering over to sample a slice of the delicious pavlova everyone was praising, when her glance slid across to where Dusty sat eating with a woman and man about his own age, an older lady and a boy.

Noreen noticed her gaze and said, 'That's Dusty's family — his sister Sally, and her husband Phil Barnes, and their little man Oliver. Dusty and Sally's mother Elizabeth is at the far end, but everyone calls her Beth. There's another daughter Sophie, lives in South Australia. Right tomboy she always was. Owns half of a sheep station in the Flinders Ranges. The family all keep pretty close since the accident. Dusty's such a fine-looking outback man,' she sighed, 'but women don't have much luck there. He's still grieving for his dead wife.'

'Oh.' Jolted by the sudden distressing news, Meghan saw Dusty in a whole new light. Suddenly she appreciated that air of sadness and mystery that clung to him, and was filled with a tug of disappointment that his heart still staunchly clung to another soul.

'What happened?'

'Car accident two years ago in the middle of the night on a long straight stretch of road.' Noreen flashed her a telling glance that clearly conveyed the reality of remote living and the necessity of driving great distances. 'Far as they could tell, she fell asleep at the wheel, spun out in gravel at the roadside and rolled.' Meghan gasped. 'Alison Nash was an ambitious achiever,' Noreen continued reverently, 'working long hours, travelling long distances. More often away from the property than on it. But Dusty adored her and supported her career. Must have made it difficult for the young couple though.'

It was taking him a long time to deal with his grief, Meghan reflected, and realised the tragedy could explain many things. 'Any children?'

Noreen shook her head. 'Such a shame

and a waste of a young life, not to mention the sorrow for those left behind. His father, Beth's husband Dan, died, oh . . . ' She frowned in thought for a moment. ' . . . it must be about ten years ago now. Beth's a keen gardener and they open up their Sunday Plains gardens and homestead for the annual charity fundraiser in spring. She moved into town when Dusty married four years ago but she often travels out there.' Meghan noticed a small thoughtful smile play over Noreen's mouth. 'He was named after his dad of course, but I've never known anyone to call him Daniel. Since he was a boy, he's always been known as Dusty.'

'Was his wife a local?'

'Alison?' Noreen vigorously shook her head. 'Good heavens no. Perth girl. Bit of an eye-opener it was, too. Dusty went down to the city on business, met Alison, fell for her and convinced her to marry him. Dusty was that proud of her and it was plain they were very much in love.'

It surprised Meghan to learn that another woman had so deeply captured his heart. He didn't seem the type to easily give it away. All the more heartbreaking for him to lose his wife, and his inability apparently so far in letting go. Hard to imagine such an outwardly rugged person being cut so hard inside. It gave her brief pause to reflect on Dermot and how she would feel in similar circumstances. Devastated for sure, and it would take some getting over.

'Alison was a marketing professional. She helped midwest station owners with branding and image, doing their newsletters, advertising, website development, that sort of thing,' Noreen went on. 'Taking their products out to the world with events and expos, finding markets, expanding exports. She still kept a core business in Perth and was always driving into Geraldton and then flying down to the city for a few days to see clients. She was such an energetic person.'

And one, Meghan knew now, it was proving hard to forget. Her frowning gaze wandered in Dusty's direction again and her heart went out to him that he soon found peace of mind and personal closure. Without it, he could never move on.

Noreen rose to her feet. 'Well I'm off to see if they need another pair of hands in the kitchen.'

'Do you need my help?'

'Good heavens no, girl.' Noreen laid a firm hand on her shoulder. 'It's your first night here and you're the guest of honour. They'll be asking you to volunteer for all kinds of things soon enough.' She laughed and disappeared into the crowd.

Meghan noticed a few individuals gather at the front of the hall. Someone tapped a glass and there was a call to order. Gazes turned in her direction and she realised this was Mallawa's version of official speeches. A local shire councillor, John Edwards, introduced himself. 'You were a strong contender right from the start, Meghan, with your glowing references. It also helped that you were a country girl from a small town who loves riding horses and sports. We can always do with more players on the local teams.' He winked and everyone chuckled before a rowdy round of applause.

Dusty rose to speak, too. 'John has welcomed our new teacher on behalf of the shire and I'm sure Barbara will have welcoming words at school. But as chairman of the community support committee who helped make our selection from the applicants, I would like to welcome Meghan into the district.' He paused and glanced directly at her. 'I'm sure one of the local lads will volunteer to help teach you how to change a tyre.'

Meghan wanted to say *I'd rather it was you* but just grinned amid the general rumble of humour that flowed around the hall and the embarrassed nudges among the likely males present.

School principal Barbara Hunter concluded the speeches by briefly adding a few succinct words to the mix. 'We've already had a long chat on Skype, Meghan. We're all excited to see you at school for your first day on Monday. I trust some of the parents have made themselves known,' she hinted, smiling, 'and we all hope you spend an enjoyable and rewarding semester among us.'

Finally Meghan rose and scanned the faces, some of whom were already familiar. One in particular, but she forced her gaze to stop wandering in his direction. 'Thank you all so much for your warmth and friendship already. I love my house and all the touches you've put into it for me. There's such a strong sense of community here, like my home town back in Ireland, so I'm really looking forward to being part of it all while I'm here and meeting the children and their families. I applied for this position to expand my horizons and because I've learned that challenging myself makes me a stronger person. You all live in a powerful corner of the world out here and it sounds like most of you know and treasure it. You all know where I live and anyone's welcome to drop in for a chinwag.'

The completion of the formalities seemed to signal the green light of approval, for Meghan was suddenly besieged with locals approaching and making introductions. Families with children were the first to leave. The younger district men congregated out on the oval, their loud voices and deep laughter carrying through the wide-open doors and into the hall. No one seemed to mind the crisp chill of night air wafting in. Others stood around a blazing log fire outdoors.

As the crowd thinned and the evening drew to a close, Meghan waved off the last of the smiling parents and friendly children who had inspected their new teacher, including some beautiful dark-skinned Aboriginal youngsters with beaming smiles, white teeth and a shy manner about them.

The core of volunteer women returned

from the kitchen nursing mugs of tea and settled in a communal circle for a chat. They beckoned Meghan to join them. Someone found her a chair and Noreen handed her a slip of paper. 'The pavlova recipe.'

'Thanks.'

Dusty's sister Sally caught her eye across the hall. She smiled, turned to her mother Beth, pointed in her direction and they wandered over, trailed by a small boy sleepily rubbing his eyes.

'Welcome to Mallawa, Meghan,' Sally said, sitting nearby. 'Since Noreen's already cornered you, you probably already know who we are.' She chuckled.

Meghan nodded, admiring the lovely young woman so like her brother except for shorter cropped hair streaked blonde from the sun but with the same casual waves.

'This is my mother, Beth Nash.'

'It's nice to meet you, dear.' The gracious woman leant forward and smiled. Her styled grey hair still held wisps of brown running through. Her manner suggested more than a hint of refinement, but beneath the facade she was still an outback woman and settled in easily among her fellow locals. Like mother, like son, Meghan mused, for Dusty Nash wore a quiet air of distinction about him, too.

'I'm married to Phil,' Sally continued. 'He was our neighbour growing up on Bindi station. We always had camp-outs and stock musters together, especially in school holidays, so I've married my very best mate and Dusty's best friend,' she said warmly.

Meghan experienced a quiet wave of envy for the woman's clear affection for her husband. Pity it didn't always follow that someone you grew up with remained dear in your life. Thoughts of Dermot briefly flashed across her mind and it surprised her to discover that she found it a relief to be free of him for a while.

'This is our son, Ollie.' Meghan refocused as Sally went on.

'Hiya, Ollie.' She judged him to be

about six or seven, and he had a mop of thick blonde hair. Ollie gave a shy grin but remained silent. 'I'm not sure what students I'll be teaching but I look forward to seeing you at school.'

'He stays with Grandma Beth during the week because we live so far out. He could do School of the Air through Meekathara, but with no brothers or sisters and while he's still young, we thought it better for him to get to know some friends his own age. It's so handy having Mum in town and she loves having his company. Sometimes she drives out on a Friday night to bring him home.' She fondled her son's curly hair. 'Other times we take a run in to fetch him and do the fortnightly stock-up.'

'So you're a fair way out, then?'

'Another half hour east beyond Dusty on Sunday Plains, so it's a two-hour drive.'

Meghan's interest sharpened at yet another lovely-sounding property name. 'It's grand of you to come in so far for the barbeque this evening.'

'Our pleasure.' She wrinkled her nose. 'Good excuse for socialising. We're all staying with Mum for the weekend.'

'Your brother was certainly a lifesaver when I was stuck out on the road this afternoon. Sounds like I'm going to have to learn how to change a tyre.'

'Wise woman. Everyone needs to be self-reliant out here.' Ollie yawned and Sally hugged him close. 'Well, young man, we best get home to Grandma's, hmm? Time for bed.' She rose. 'Nice to meet you, Meghan.'

'You, too.'

'I'm sure Mum or Dusty could bring you out to visit of a weekend. If you want,' she added hastily, perhaps noting Meghan's surprise and hesitation.

'Oh, I'd not want to be troubling anyone.'

'Nonsense. They'd be happy to do it and I'd love the company. Besides, Sunday Plains and Bindi both have horses,' she coaxed with a playful grin.

'How could I resist then?' Meghan

laughed. 'It's a date, but give me time to settle in.'

'Sure. We'll see you around.'

Beth murmured a polite good night and they left. Some of Ollie's drowsiness must have rubbed off on her because she fought a yawn. To her embarrassment, as she glanced around, her gaze was trapped by Dusty, amusement on his face. *Jaysus*. She cringed. *Has he caught me with my mouth wide open?*

He strolled over in his usual easy way. 'You've had a long day. Time to split.' He took her elbow and steered her across the hall, weaving among the last few drinkers and stayers, heading for the door.

Back at Meghan's house, for no particular logical reason she could justify, she felt compelled to let Dusty know she'd learned about Alison. So beneath the porch in the semi-darkness, since he had insisted on walking with her from the car, she turned a direct gaze on him. 'Noreen mentioned you lost your wife.' His jaw clenched and he stiffened. She laid a hand gently on his jacket sleeve. 'I'm sorry,' she said softly. 'None of us has any guarantees in life, but it's especially hard when it's someone young.'

Since it was common knowledge that he remained vulnerable even after two years, Meghan simply acknowledged his loss since his emotions were still raw, and she moved the conversation on. 'Some barbeque,' she said lightly. 'A grand night. I hope Mallawa has lots of those.'

'Can guarantee it.'

'Sally said Sunday Plains is quite a way out of town.'

He nodded. 'About an hour.'

'How on earth did you get the name?'

'Nothing original.' He sank his hands into his pockets and shrugged. 'My great-grandfather Benjamin Nash arrived on the property on a Sunday. You've seen how flat the country, is so you can work out the rest.'

Despite his reticence, tragic recent

41

background and distance from town, Meghan genuinely hoped she saw more of this man. 'Thank you for taking care of me today.'

'Don't forget to have that tyre repaired. If you have another flat, you'll be needing it. There's only one garage in town.'

She nodded. 'Sure. I'll see to it.

'Night,' he murmured after a decent hesitation, then dissolved into the gloomy night.

Meghan found herself staring off into the dark long after he was gone.

3

Meghan woke slowly and stretched, then snuggled under the doona, adapting her thoughts to her new surroundings. The clock told her half the morning was gone already thanks to jetlag, so she padded out to the living room in her pyjamas and bed socks to light the fire.

She pulled on leggings, a thick warm sloppy jumper, and her runners ready for a jog after breakfast. Staggered by the bountiful contents of the refrigerator and pantry, Meghan christened her cooker by scrambling fresh eggs and chopped herbs with crispy bacon and eating it on her lap in front of the fire, followed by a mug of hot tea. Then she tied back her mass of hair, wrapped on her favourite black woolly scarf and headed out onto the deserted streets. Meghan found herself waving to the few residents about and had her greetings returned.

She set herself an easy pace so she could have a good look at everything. A dog chased her for a time until its owner whistled it back. She found the school and stood at the fence, doing leg stretches while she gave it an eyeful. New orderly buildings reflected community pride despite Mallawa's remote location. Meghan's interest was captured by panels of stunning Aboriginal artwork painted in rich earthy colours on some exterior walls. She looked forward to learning more about the indigenous culture.

She had already jogged past the town's impressive sporting complex, solar-heated swimming pool and basketball courts. The locals were certainly proactive to achieve such amenities out here. She opted for a quick lap of the recreation oval, then curiosity won out to retrace her steps and explore the cemetery she had noticed earlier on the edge of town.

As she reached it, Meghan pulled up

sharply when she recognised Dusty's four-wheel drive parked by the front fence. The central gate swung open. Raising a hand, she squinted to see more clearly against the brilliant sunshine. She held back when she noticed him hunkered down before a grave, deeply absorbed in his homage. Of course. His wife. He placed a bunch of greenery in a vase holder then stood, twirling his big hat in his hands and gazing off into the distance. Meghan tactfully retreated to jog around a nearby block of houses and return later.

When she reappeared within ten minutes, Dusty was gone. She pushed open the wrought-iron gate and strolled in the direction of Dusty's visit. The cemetery ambience was peaceful except for the excited shrieking of flashing red and green birds squabbling in the perimeter gum trees. Meghan stilled. They were so bright and beautiful. Birds back home weren't nearly as colourful.

Within moments Meghan found what she sought. He had left lavender.

A liberal and riotous dried bunch of it plunged casually into the vase. Meghan reached down and rubbed a knob of the pungent perfumed herb between her fingers. The significance of the gesture was not lost on her. Lavender for remembrance. Somehow while Dusty Nash was still alive, she doubted his wife would ever be forgotten.

Behind, the gleaming silver headstone was inscribed in black. *Alison Caroline Nash, loved wife of Dusty, accidentally killed.* Then the date. Meghan sucked in a quick breath as she read further. *Only child of Roger and Sheryl Winters.* How doubly sad.

Two steps further on was another Nash grave, equally well tended. *Daniel Benjamin Nash.* Dusty's father and Beth's husband, she presumed. Noting the date ten years prior, his son must have assumed the reins of Sunday Plains at a young age. She judged Dusty to be about her own age, which meant he would have been barely twenty.

Meghan wandered on, loosening her

scarf as the morning warmed, and found herself in the older part of the cemetery among pioneer graves. Drunken headstones and barely legible wording told their own story. A labourer had died when a rope broke and he fell into a well; another from a wheat-loader accident. Gunshot wounds. A goldsmith from heart failure. Pneumonia.

Contemplating precious life stirred her first notions toward a resolution with Dermot. She hadn't heard from him and wondered if he'd even bother. He'd had a right puss on him when she'd left. He'd expect her to contact him first. The stubborn fiancée coming to her senses and begging his forgiveness. She scowled over the unlikely possibility and ran for home. He'd need to be showing a more healthy respect for her feelings and opinions before that happened. No. She would wait. Dermot O'Brien could make the first move. If he truly loved and wanted her, he could prove it. Meanwhile, she would focus on enjoying her time in Mallawa.

★ ★ ★

On Monday morning Meghan drove to school, arriving early for a prearranged preliminary briefing with Principal Barbara Hunter. She received smiles and shy waves from those children she already knew from the Saturday night barbeque as she crossed the school grounds.

'Morning,' she greeted as she entered the main building to find her superior waiting.

'Meghan, hello. Stay on your feet. We'll do a quick tour.' This entailed a brisk patrol of the classrooms, the library, and the music and arts wing.

Passing the home economics room, Meghan admitted, 'I'd love to help in there.'

Barbara nodded. 'Noted.' Then she indicated raised garden beds in a sheltered courtyard. 'Beth Nash administers that area and helps co-ordinate volunteers to come in and work and teach the children.'

As they steered around students in

48

the long, wide hallways, Meghan admired Barbara's firm command and genial manner. She was middle-aged and single, apparently devoting her life to her career. While Meghan loved her work, she knew that would never be enough. Her love of children meant she longed to be a mother herself one day, although Dermot wanted to delay. Pushing thirty, she disagreed, and once again they had clashed.

'It's NAIDOC week next month.' Barbara set an efficient pace which mirrored the character of the person behind the long strides. 'National Aboriginal and Islander Day observance,' she explained. 'A day of remembrance for Aboriginal people and their heritage. You'll learn a lot. It's a colourful week.'

'I love the Aboriginal art on your buildings.'

She beamed proudly. 'Our talented secondary students are responsible. Being an independent public school, we can set and monitor our curriculum to best cater for our students' needs, but we're still part of the public school system. That's one of the reasons why we applied to employ you to work one-to-one with individual children.'

'I'll enjoy that. Every child is special. Their whole life and future can be influenced by their school years.'

'We're on the same page, then.' Barbara smiled. 'Independent schools do need to take greater responsibility for their affairs, but ultimately we feel it benefits all students. As you know, we draw heavily on community support and volunteers such as Noreen in the library and Beth with gardening.'

Meghan was inspired. Then the bell siren sounded and there was a general scramble of children heading outdoors. 'Monday is assembly,' Barbara explained as she led Meghan from the building. 'We have a small ceremony where we raise both the Australian and Aboriginal flags, and play our national anthem. We present awards.' She paused. 'And introduce new teachers,' she said with a grin. 'So stay close.'

Meghan was immediately drawn into her first day at her new school. She felt cheerful at the prospect of a fresh outlook in her professional and private lives. After school, she did as Dusty had nagged and dropped off her punctured tyre at the garage. A burly fella named Gazza with a face full of whiskers hauled it from the boot and rolled it away. She arranged to collect it next day.

The sunny midwest days and cold nights moved into each other and her first week flew. She mastered her cooker and found that friends, neighbours and fellow teachers dropped by as much to socialise for a drink and conversation as to eat her food. Especially once word spread about her cooking.

Kindergarten teacher Carrie Edwards was a mad keen photographer renowned for heading out before daybreak and stomping through the landscape in her thick hiking boots to catch the golden early morning sunlight, usually on weekends. When her insulated travel mug of coffee emptied and hunger growled, she arrived at Meghan's house unannounced and parked her well-loved but aged four-wheel drive at the kerb and begged breakfast.

The first time when Meghan had served up the full Irish of eggs, sausages, bacon, tomato and potato farls, even foodie Carrie had protested in horror. 'I can't eat all that! It's a day's calories in one sitting.' But over a chinwag she had scraped her plate clean, including the juices, with a slice of fried bread.

Meghan could only laugh. 'In the pub back home one old fella calls it a heart attack on a plate, but he's over eighty now so his big Sunday breakfast once a week doesn't seem to have done him much harm.'

As promised every week, one of the rota of CWA ladies bustled in the back door straight into Meghan's kitchen and made themselves at home. Fortunately, it was often of an evening when she was weary after a day's teaching and appreciated the gesture. Meghan loved lifting the lids on casseroles and cake containers to investigate what was inside.

She returned the favour by doing what she loved: baking. Thick slices of barm brack spread with butter. Her special Guinness chocolate cake that always disappeared fast, and her apple cinnamon cake. A fat glass jar on the kitchen counter was always full of oatmeal biscuits. Carrie was known to grab a handful to go before heading out the back door after one of her visits. Meghan soon learned that the Australian equivalent of Anzac biscuits went down a treat, too, after Noreen gave her the recipe.

When it was Beth Nash's turn, Meghan was particularly pleased. She admired the strong, competent country woman as much for her motherly graciousness as her straightforward attitude to life and getting things done. But she was also awed by the aristocratic air she conveyed. They talked about the school garden, the spring flowers and vegetable seedlings coming on in the greenhouse, the children's excitement at watching them grow, and Beth's enjoyment of the shared experience doing what she loved and passing on her knowledge.

'Is the family all well?' Meghan asked when the conversation lapsed while they shared a cuppa across the kitchen table, genuinely interested but with a sneaky motive in her mind.

Beth nodded. 'The men have started cropping. Makes it hard when Dusty's out working a long day,' she continued, 'and he comes in after dark at some crazy hour having to get a meal. He's never been much in the kitchen, and Alison was away a lot.' Her concentration faltered but she gathered her thoughts and smiled fondly. 'He always did prefer the outdoors, and he doesn't eat as well as he should. I've been cooking all week to restock his freezer so he has some decent meals on hand. I'm heading out to Sunday Plains to deliver it all.' She hesitated and regarded

Meghan carefully. 'Sally phoned this morning and wondered if you'd like to go out to Bindi for a weekend visit and some riding. I'm taking Ollie home on Friday after school, so you could come along as a passenger. Only if you're free,' she added cautiously.

Excited by an opportunity to see Sally and Dusty again, Meghan hesitated because it sounded like Beth was hoping she'd refuse. 'You probably want to spend time catching up after a busy week though,' Beth excused quickly, standing.

Since Sally made the invitation, Meghan decided the prospect overcame her caution. 'No, not at all. I'd love it, actually.'

Beth's face clouded. 'Are you sure? It's a long drive out there.'

'Absolutely.' Meghan smiled her pleasure. 'I haven't ridden in ages. I'd welcome the chance.'

Beth's friendly manner cooled and she moved for the door. 'I'll pick you up at five Friday night, then.'

Naturally after that, the week dragged.

Meghan looked forward to seeing Dusty again, although it would only be briefly as they called in on their way to Bindi. Plus there was the anticipation of riding again. But her excitement was dimmed when she received two phone calls from Ireland.

The first one spoiled the rest of the week. Meghan had just tossed her car keys onto the kitchen counter after a busy school day and was heading for the living room to light the fire for the evening when her mobile rang. She paused in shock to read the caller ID. Finally, after two weeks. She drew in a deep breath, wondering what would follow.

'Dermot.' She tried to sound pleased to cover her apprehension at his attitude during this first contact since she'd left Ireland. Hardly the doting fiancé anymore. The change had her puzzled, so she waited for his reason. 'It's good to hear from you.' What else could she say until he revealed his position and the conversation developed?

'Meghan.' He sounded stern, the

only one among her close family and friends who refused to use her nickname of Meggie.

She scrambled to think what time it might be back home. Morning? 'Are you at work?' she asked lightly.

'Of course. Have been for hours. It's after nine already.'

So, he was still angry and clearly didn't intend to make this easy or pleasant. Meghan's disappointment washed through her in waves. He was still unprepared to meet her halfway. Didn't all their years together count for more effort between them to try and salvage what scraps of feeling and commitment remained? At least from him. Or had he actually become detached about their relationship now, too? She frowned. Something didn't feel right. He sounded too indifferent and not his usual enthusiastic conceited self. A vast change compared to the heated objections when she announced she was coming to Australia.

This start to their conversation was so uncomfortable and stilted, it reminded her of that first meeting with Dusty. Meghan pulled up her thoughts. Now what had suddenly brought him to mind? Power of suggestion maybe, because she would be seeing him this weekend? Dermot was speaking so she snapped her attention back. Whatever he was saying, his tone dripped with indignation and complaint.

'I've tried contacting you but whenever I was free, it's been some ungodly hour over there.'

Jumping straight in with the criticisms again. No asking if she was fine and telling her he missed her. 'The time zones *can* prove awkward,' she said mildly. 'But there's nothing we can do about it.'

'I'm sure you deliberately chose so far away just to make it difficult.' His tone was laced with resentment.

Meghan let his unfair disapproval slide for a moment and drew in a slow, calming breath before responding. 'Actually, it wouldn't have mattered where the job was,' she admitted. 'It appealed and I wanted a change.'

'Is this cold feet before we marry?' he challenged.

Well, nothing like being direct. 'I'm reassessing *us*, Dermot, as I plainly told you before I left. For now, I can't offer you more than that. You know we've not been as compatible or close this year.'

'We'd be perfectly fine if you'd take my advice,' he snapped.

'Your ideals aren't necessarily right for me.' They had revisited this conversation so many times it felt like listening to a recording.

'I have a wealth of business career strategy and management experience. I could help you go far.'

More like *drive* me far. Away, Meghan thought, with a sense of hopeless inevitability. Maybe she'd made a mistake and should have stayed in Ireland and sorted it out between them. Except after only a few weeks apart she was beginning to realise they had little to rescue.

His relentless attempts to mould her to the person he wanted her to be were growing thin. She'd begun to feel trapped. Meghan just wanted to be loved for herself and spread her wings in her own way and in the direction she chose. Her frustration had only surged in recent months at Dermot's need to improve her. She feared she no longer met his expectations of the woman he wanted beside him.

'Everyone wants to succeed.' Dermot drove home his point.

'Is my being a teacher not achievement enough for you or worth anything for its own sake?' she appealed, feeling bleak.

His sudden silence was odd, for Dermot was never lost for words. Had she hit upon the crux of her deficiency in his eyes? She was no longer good enough to complement his own rising accomplishments? Wounded by his unspoken implication, Meghan took offence not only for herself but all the dedicated teachers of the world trying to give the best possible education and opportunity to all the children and students on the planet. To help fulfil their purpose and achieve their dreams and potential. Without even a basic education, children were disadvantaged.

Her heart wrenched with indignity on their behalf and ached a little at Dermot's narrow-minded view. Meghan sensed the pointless direction of the conversation and reflected on her new inner peace even after a few short weeks of distance from this man with whom she now always seemed to clash. She marvelled they had stayed together so long. But worse, what had she been thinking to become engaged to him?

Because, a small nagging voice whispered in her head, *you gave in as always, rejecting your intuition when you should have walked away.*

Their discussions always sank to this bickering. Meghan questioned why Dermot had even bothered to call. Eventually. Obligation? Some warped belief that she would change her mind, was missing him madly and would be on the first flight home? In fact, she'd hardly thought of him at all and felt only slightly guilty for the lapse. No sense continuing the call. They were getting nowhere.

'Dermot?' She frowned over the quiet line.

'Sorry Meghan, I had to take another call.'

Naturally. Business always came first. Their inattention to each other spoke more loudly than any words. Meghan had gone off daydreaming and Dermot hadn't even been on the line! She closed her eyes and shook her head in frustration. She hadn't even particularly cared that he'd taken the trouble out of his busy, important day to call. She knew nothing would change. She just hadn't faced it yet.

'I should let you go then,' Meghan said lamely. 'Why *did* you call?' she urged, bitten with mischief and waited with interest to hear his reply.

'To see how you are.'

'Oh. You forgot to ask me that.' Dermot hated criticism but he loved to serve it up. 'Do you still want to know?'

'You sound fine,' he snapped.

'Yes, I am. I'm just grand.'

She didn't elaborate about the wonderful friends she'd made so soon, the excitement and challenge of her new teaching environment. The quiet seduction of the outback, as much to do with the warmth of its people as the special sense of place. If there wasn't a dollar in it, Dermot wouldn't be interested.

They managed half-hearted good-byes, both promising to keep in touch but neither truly meaning it, Meghan suspected. Their contact would likely trickle away to nothing. After he hung up, she stared at the mobile in her hand, filled with regret that the childhood friend who had turned into her mentor and then become her fiancé was now slipping from her life. She was not heartless. She wished it could have been different and they could have worked it out; but from where she stood in her life at the moment, she knew that those first heady feelings had evaporated and fickle love had dissolved before her eyes.

With a sense of calm acceptance, Meghan realised she would only briefly feel the loss. Somewhere at some time in the future, probably when she returned home for Christmas if Dermot didn't push it beforehand, they would need to talk. Face it. End it.

She had only worn his exquisite personally designed solitaire diamond ring for two weeks. It *had* looked rather fantastic on her hand for a while, but she had left it nestled among ivory velvet in its box back home.

Two days later the second phone call came from Ireland. Claire. Complaining because she was never on Skype.

'I'm busy, eejit,' Meghan teased. 'I do work for a living, you know.'

'The time difference doesn't help. When I'm sleeping you're awake,' she moaned.

Where had Meghan heard that before? Claire's grumbles made her feel even lower. Chinwags with her friend were usually cheery. This conversation was starting out as scratchy as the one with Dermot.

Meghan sighed and tried again. 'Do you want to hang up and Skype instead? I can go and turn on my laptop.'

Half the time she didn't bother anymore. After her early-morning run, teaching all day, visitors and baking, life was pleasantly full, she realised. Meghan hadn't reflected on her easy transition and inclusion into the community. And Noreen's forewarning of being swept up into volunteering was proving true. Already she was being drawn into special preparations for NAIDOC week.

'No,' Claire said, 'we'll just keep it short. It's costing a fortune.'

'I offered.' Meghan grew irritated.

'You did,' Claire conceded.

'So, how's everything back home?' Meghan asked brightly.

'Well, it's hardly all laughs, I can tell you. Dermot had a right puss on him last weekend. Went down the pub and grumbled to your parents about you.'

Meghan gasped in astonishment. 'Of all the nerve. He's already had a crack at me.'

'He asked them to talk sense into you.'

Meghan's mother knew her feelings for Dermot had cooled. They'd had a confidential chat before she left.

'So how's it going with that big handsome outback man, then?'

Claire's query came out of nowhere and Meghan smiled. 'Apart from the day he rescued me out on the road, I've not seen him,' she admitted.

Her arrival seemed so long ago now already. She didn't elaborate on the welcome barbeque or mention her sighting of Dusty at the cemetery. She cautiously withheld the information, feeling disloyal to Dermot for fancying another man. With an effort, she said, 'So, it's Friday night. Have you made any plans?'

'Just the usual. Going out with the girls.'

Meghan considered their mutual group of friends and wondered what they would make of this vast midwest. Mostly they were city girls, eager to escape town and head for Dublin for some craic. They might enjoy it here for a while but not for long. At the moment, Meghan felt like she could stay forever. She hoped the novelty didn't fade, for she was loving it here. Of course that could have something to do with Dermot's absence, but despite the isolation she already had heaps of friends and support.

'What *do* you get up to out in the bush over there?' Claire asked in an edgy tone.

Was her friend bitter, too, because she'd up and left? She hadn't considered how her lifelong friend might react. She only knew it had been important to claim time and space to herself to evaluate what truly lay in her heart and what she wanted for her future. After Dermot's phone call, her future path was becoming apparent.

'Usually not much,' Meghan confessed, although her life felt anything but dull. 'But as it happens I've been invited out to a property a couple hours from town this weekend. A friend, Sally, has horses so I'm hoping to go riding.'

'You'll like that. You're a one for the outdoors.'

Claire chattered on about people they knew but Meghan felt removed from the gossip. Her friend soon brought the call to an end, moaning about the cost, and Meghan hung up, feeling disappointed.

4

'We haven't rushed you?' Beth checked as she bustled into Meghan's kitchen on Friday evening, Ollie trailing wide-eyed behind her.

'Not at all,' she promised, assessing the older woman's neat jeans and rugby top, pleased to be similarly dressed herself. 'I've packed my toughest gear and I'm really looking forward to the weekend.'

'The track's unsealed once we leave the main road out of town but we should be at Sunday Plains within the hour. Then it's another half hour to Bindi.'

'I have my international licence if you need a spell away from the wheel,' Meghan offered.

'I've being driving the track for forty years,' Beth said bluntly. 'I'm sure I'll manage.'

Meghan pulled back, hurt at her

sharp tone, wondering what she'd done wrong to offend the woman since arriving and failing to find an answer.

As they sped north from town in silence, Meghan sensed Beth grow more relaxed behind the wheel. Maybe Beth been rushed before they left, she thought forgivingly, which accounted for her prickly behaviour.

The lowering sun to their left spread pastel streaks across the sky and the vehicle threw out a thin swirl of dust behind. Meghan sensed a buoyant anticipation in her fellow travellers to be heading home. Despite the rough gravel road dictating slower speeds, they made good time. In the companionable silence, conversation proved mostly unnecessary.

Closer to their destination and to Meghan's surprise, Beth finally spoke. 'You're seeing the country at its greenest now, but in spring the entire landscape as far as you can see is covered with wildflowers. Especially everlastings. By the end of July, wattles start coming out.'

'I read about them,' Meghan said. 'It promises to be a wonderful sight.'

Beth cast her a glance of grudging approval. 'The whole state comes alive with tourists from all over the world and trekkers doing the north during winter in their campers and mobile homes. They'll be mostly in the far north and the territory at the moment,' she explained, 'but they head south again come spring. September is the main month. That's when we open up Sunday Plains gardens. We usually schedule it for during the school holidays so families can participate and help. It's one of our major fundraisers for the year. Any later and the gardens are past their best and the whole district is buzzing with harvest anyway. I've heard you like cooking,' she ventured carefully. 'Perhaps you could help us out with some baking?'

Meghan nodded. 'Of course.'

'The committee would appreciate it. We serve hundreds of afternoon teas under the verandas and trees.'

'How big is Sunday Plains?'

'It started at the last cattle ramp about ten minutes back. This is the road across the property into the homestead. There are only fences around the main paddocks and the property boundaries.' She shrugged. 'I guess it's roughly about twenty thousand acres or eight thousand hectares.'

Meghan gasped. 'You're letting on?'

'We're going to have to educate our new teacher, Ollie, aren't we?' she said abruptly, half turning toward her grandson in the back seat.

He chuckled and glanced out of the window. 'Yeah. We're nearly at Uncle Dusty's place.'

Twilight lingered as night settled. In the remaining daylight, signs of civilisation gradually came into view. A barely stirring windmill, a long-open fronted shed filled with farm machinery, harvesters and trucks. A row of round steel bins.

'What are those?' Meghan asked.

'Grain silos,' Ollie piped up cheerfully.

'Not much our young man doesn't know about farming out here already,' Beth said with smug grandmotherly pride.

Then the homestead itself and surrounding trees loomed into view. Meghan sighed. It was like an oasis in the desert. 'It's so green,' she marvelled.

'Well, it's winter,' Beth said crisply as she steered them through the narrow open gateway and they rumbled over the final cattle grid. 'But we have dams, bores and the good fortune of a soak.'

Meghan frowned.

'A natural spring,' she explained. 'Dan's grandfather, Ben Nash, chose the location well for his family and descendants out here. His first home was a tent.'

And then they were sweeping around the circular gravelled driveway to pull up before the homestead, a huge square white timbered dwelling with broad verandas on all sides. On the expansive lawns at the front, huge big old eucalypts stretched their fat and curving ancient limbs in all directions in open-armed welcome. Peppercorn trees, familiar to Meghan from street plantings in town, draped their ferny trailing branches to the ground beneath. The whole surroundings were neat and tidy. Clearly a beloved home.

But the most stimulating aspect of the scenery was the imposing man in jeans, checked shirt, black leather jerkin and sturdy black boots standing with his hands on his hips waiting on the broad front steps, his expression serious but quiet, and looking the comfortable master of his kingdom. Two beautiful black and white border collies sat obediently on their haunches beside him. Meghan's spirits lifted to see him again.

When she could tear it away, her gaze was drawn by banks of clipped lavender edging the garden beds that would no doubt send their aromatic perfume in musky drifts across the garden throughout spring and summer. She wished for more daylight at this late hour so she could have a clearer view of it all.

Ollie scrambled out of his seatbelt and was out the door before Beth had turned off the engine. At the barest nod from their master, the dogs left the veranda and the boy embraced them both before sending an admiring glance at the man now ambling from the house toward them.

'Hey, Uncle Dusty.'

He grinned and affectionately ruffled the boy's blond hair. Then his slow gaze moved in Meghan's direction as she emerged from the vehicle to stretch. 'Meghan. Good to see you again.'

'You, too.' They politely shook hands. Her skin tingled from his touch and the warmth of his handshake. 'It's powerful country out here,' she said with genuine enthusiasm.

His eyes glinted with pride. 'We think so.'

He warmly hugged his mother and pressed a gentle kiss on her forehead when she quietly appeared at his side. The affectionate gesture and unguarded moment encouraged Meghan that a loving heart still beat in this rugged, troubled man.

'Dusty, dear, can you help me lift the freezer box before we go?' Beth asked.

'Sure.' He raised the rear door and easily hauled his mother's supplies inside. 'Come on in for a moment, Meghan,' he said over his shoulder.

The dogs fussed excitedly around her ankles as Meghan followed the others indoors, deeply curious to see the house where Dusty lived.

'Queenie, Butch. Sit,' he commanded. The beautiful dogs instantly obeyed and waited, hopeful, outside looking in, their heads tilted appealingly to one side.

Meghan let the screen door slam shut behind her and reverently absorbed her surroundings. Sunday Plains homestead was comfortable and immaculate. Clearly Dusty had some kind of domestic help if he worked out on his property all day. Polished timber floors gleamed. Long carpet runners in the broad hallway ran through the house.

Trailing after the family, Meghan emerged into a huge country kitchen and released a long sigh of pleasure. Now *this* was a kitchen. Dusty was already unloading foil containers into his freezer in one half of an enormous refrigerator and Ollie clambered up onto a stool at the central island bench, swinging his short legs.

While everyone was preoccupied, Meghan crossed her arms and tried to look casual as she discreetly glanced around. Wide windows above the sink and counters looked out across the rear garden to the distant horizon. With daylight almost gone, only a hovering greyness remained as night fell.

Double French doors led out onto a covered patio with a table, chairs and huge barbeque. They didn't do things by halves out here. It might be located at the heart of the property and seemingly in the middle of nowhere, but to Meghan's amazement Sunday Plains homestead had every comfort and convenience. She stood aside quietly, surprised and impressed by the well-appointed fittings and homely atmosphere.

Beth and Dusty finished unloading the food. He pressed the portable freezer-box lid back on. 'Here, muscles.' He pushed it toward Ollie. 'Take this out to Grandma's car before we leave.'

We? Meghan shook her head. What had she missed?

'The powder room is through the laundry to your left if you want it,' he suggested tactfully.

She flashed a quick smile. 'I'm fine.'

How could she have been so daft? Except for Dusty, the entire family would be gathered at Sally's for the weekend. So why would he stay home here alone? Across the kitchen, Dusty caught her eye. Like a wild animal caught in head-lights, Meghan was unable to look away.

'I'll get my overnight bag,' he murmured, holding her gaze. 'Mum, I'll drive, okay?'

'Of course.' She dropped the keys into his hand.

Meghan felt deflated at Beth's easy way with her son. She knew Sally's invitation for the weekend was genuine, but she still felt like an intruder around their mother.

'If we're all ready?' he prompted and Meghan somehow made her feet move toward the hall and out the door.

Ollie was waiting by the car, playing with the dogs. They trotted loyally around Dusty as he appeared.

'Meghan, you stay in the front seat,' he insisted. 'Mum can keep Ollie company in the back.'

'Are you sure?' She glanced between them. 'You must both have heaps to talk about.'

'We have the whole weekend for that,' he murmured generously.

Dusty's gentle glance rested on her at length, like a silent reaching out of appeal. It felt like a barrier crumbled down between them. Meghan hid her pleasure because Beth glared but, from that brief exchange, she was forced to consider the possibility that Dusty Nash was casually interested in her. She couldn't deny her own returning fascination. How had that happened? More to the point, when? They'd only seen each other once on the day of her arrival weeks ago. Her heart skipped with lightness, and a long list of problems tumbled over each other in her mind. For starters, she was still engaged to Dermot. And wasn't Dusty still grieving for Alison?

'Meghan?' Dusty's voice came to her softly close by. 'It's dark. We need to make tracks.' He was holding the door open.

'Yes . . . of course.'

'You were on another planet,' he observed quietly.

'I believe I was. It's all so different out here.'

She slid into the car and clicked on her seatbelt, inhaling a long, steadying breath. And then Dusty was beside her, his big strong hands firmly on the wheel. Ollie and Beth chatted amiably behind them even before he turned the key, switched on the headlights and drove back along the gravelled property road for some miles to the unsealed main road.

Five minutes later, they turned left and headed east for Bindi. Meghan wasn't confident enough to attempt conversation. She still reeled from whatever had sprung into life with Dusty back at the homestead.

After a while, he checked the rear-view mirror and grinned. 'They're both asleep back there. I'm not surprised. Mum still works hard, although she's supposed to be retired in town now, and she has the added responsibility of her grandson, too.'

'I think I can understand. As a teacher, I find every child leaves a footprint in your life.' She talked quietly so as not to wake their other passengers.

'That's a beautiful sentiment. You were clearly born to teach.'

Meghan wondered how she could have spent so little time in this man's company and yet feel so much more self-worth and harmony than she ever did with Dermot. She almost felt ashamed that she had allowed her relationship with her fiancé to develop unchecked without bothering to monitor or question its quality and evolution more closely. Now she could see its deficiency, and hadn't that been the purpose of temporarily breaking away from Ireland anyway? She was stunned how much clearer her relationship with Dermot was now, and what seemed its inevitable demise. She had expected it to take time and angst and pain.

Conversation in the car lapsed. Apart from the faint glow of lights from the dashboard, it was dark and only the vehicle headlights picked out the red gravel road ahead. Meghan must have dozed, too, but somehow the body always seemed to know when it needed to stir.

She became conscious of the vehicle engine powering down, dogs barking and Ollie exclaiming, 'We're home.'

Lights inside and out lit up Bindi homestead as if for Christmas. It was a new build in stone — probably when Sally and Phil married, Meghan guessed — with broad concrete verandas at ground level flowing directly out onto vast surrounding lawns.

Ollie was out the door and flying at his mother, wrapping his arms around her legs, all smiles and laughter. They hugged and kissed in reunion as Dusty and Beth and Meghan peeled out of the car more sedately and stretched. Dusty hauled out their overnight bags and dumped them all on the veranda.

The family hugged each other, then Phil emerged, shook hands with Dusty and bent down to kiss Beth's cheek. Their guest stood back diplomatically, barely awake, smiling at the family's joy.

'Meghan!' Sally was finally able to acknowledge her. 'Welcome to Bindi.'

'I look forward to seeing it in day-light, but I did glimpse some roos in the headlights.'

Sally laughed. 'Plenty more to see.

We'll head out on the horses in the morning but for now come on in everyone, it's freezing out here.'

She ushered them all indoors like a mother hen herding her chicks into shelter for the night.

'Something smells wonderful,' Meghan said as she stepped into the wide hall.

'Pork roast and a fruit crumble in Mum's old family baking dish. I stole it from Sunday Plains when we married. No point cooking small out here,' she was saying as the women moved into the kitchen and the men swung away into the living area. Meghan heard glasses clink and deep male laughter.

'Ollie Barnes, put your school gear away first,' Sally yelled out. They heard a groan then the shuffle of small, reluctant feet.

Being more modern, Bindi homestead was more open-plan but still with the huge country kitchen that signified the heart of any home. Sally's domain was long, with a vast central island twice the size of the one at Sunday Plains, a table seating ten at one end, and a cosy snug area with plump sofas at the other.

Within ten minutes, when Sally had carved the roast and Beth dished up the vegetables, Meghan was fully awake. Phil poured white wine and everyone took their places where they chose. There seemed to be no particular order. Understandably, Ollie stuck close to his mother and Dusty took a seat opposite. Unsettling for Meghan. It would have been easier if he had sat at her side so she wasn't confronted with those dark, dreamy eyes flashing in her direction from his strong, engaging face.

By the time they were all crunching on pork crackling and the wine glasses had been refilled, Meghan was quizzed about Mallawa, teaching at the school and how she was settling in. Her eagerness must have shone through for Dusty commented, 'It all sounds positive for you so far.'

'Yes, I'm afraid my time here is going to fly.'

'We could always apply to extend

85

your term,' Sally quipped. 'Dusty, you're on the committee,' she teased her brother. 'You could make it happen.'

'Meghan might have changed her mind by the end of the year.' He watched her closely.

She shook her head and red curls rustled about her face. She tucked one behind her ear. 'I've travelled a bit, but you soon get the measure of a place and its people. Mallawa's a powerful community and I'm loving being a part of it.'

'You haven't struck our summer yet,' Dusty cautioned.

'Trying to turn me off?' she teased.

'Never.' His eyes relayed a wealth of meaning behind the single word spoken with such warmth and promise.

Despite herself, Meghan grew hot and blushed. 'Good to know,' was all she could say lightly.

'Any of those young bucks in town offered to teach you how to change a tyre yet?' he asked.

'You make it sound like you're a

geriatric,' Meghan scoffed. 'But no, they haven't.'

'Surprising,' Sally chuckled, raising her eyebrows. 'The local lads aren't usually so slow.'

Quiet Phil grinned in the background, not saying much, Meghan noticed. Dusty glowered. He didn't seem happy about what his sister had said.

The empty plates were gathered up after the first course, then Sally produced the mammoth baking dish from the oven bubbling with fruit and juices beneath the crunchy browned crumble topping.

Meghan rose to help, watching her hostess dish up generous spoonfuls. 'So that's the famous dish.'

She served bowls to the table. A jug of thick, fresh cream arrived and little conversation took place as the diners ate every wonderful mouthful and scraped their plates.

'Sally.' Meghan glanced down to her at one end of the table. 'That was grand. Thank you.'

'You're welcome. Rumour has it you're no slouch in the kitchen either. I hope you've roped her in for the garden party in September, Mum.'

'Yes, she has kindly agreed,' Beth said politely, lacking the same joy and enthusiasm as the others around the table.

Ollie yawned. 'Time for bed, young man,' Phil said, pushing back his chair to stand.

'But I slept in the car,' he moaned.

'Nice try, buster,' his father said. 'Scoot. When you're in your pyjamas and you've done your teeth, I'll come in and read a story.' The boy brightened at the prospect and disappeared.

'Dishes can soak,' Sally announced. 'Phil will stack the washer later,' she hinted, throwing her quiet, unassuming husband a fond glance. She unlatched a glass jar of homemade biscuits, boiled the kettle, and the adults dissolved onto large sofas in the front of the open fire. Meghan found herself next to Dusty, every part of her aware of him so close. Phil withdrew to read Ollie the promised story after the boy had returned and hugged everyone good night.

Replete from the substantial dinner and entranced by the flames, Meghan only listened to the conversation among the family.

Finally Sally said, 'It's gone eleven. I'm bushed.' She uncurled from her chair. 'Meghan, I'll show you to your room. Phil's taken your bag along.'

Even though she had dozed in the car, Meghan was heavily weary, but still reluctantly rose to be deprived of Dusty at her side. Too easy to get warm and comfortable among these big-hearted people. 'Night all,' she murmured.

'Don't rise early,' Sally said as they walked down the hall of the bedroom wing. 'Ollie comes and snuggles in with us for a while on weekend mornings, so breakfast is never before nine. Especially in winter.'

'Oh, this is lovely,' Meghan gasped

when she saw the generous guest room, French doors on one wall leading directly out into the garden.

'Bathroom's next door between your room and Dusty's. Hope you don't mind sharing.'

Sally's comment was innocent enough, Meghan knew, but too much information perhaps? And some distraction to have the man of her thoughts so close.

'Good heavens, no, it's grand of you to have me.' She paused. 'If I want to go for a morning run, can you point out the right way for me? I don't want to disturb you for directions.'

'Head out any road. Stick to the tracks and you won't get lost. Come back the same way. Maybe keep the house in sight and if you have a mobile, take it with you.'

'I have. Thanks.'

'You might find some dogs along for company. Ollie's Nutmeg is a brown border collie and Clancy is brown and white and pretty much belongs to anybody who gives him attention.

They're family pets. Phil keeps the working Kelpie sheep dogs further out.'

They hugged and said good night. Meghan's head brimmed with everything she had experienced since leaving Mallawa six hours ago and the bonus surprise of Dusty's company all weekend. Thoughts of him soon had her relaxed and drifting off to sleep not long after she snuggled under the covers.

Next morning she woke to utter silence and no sound of any movement in the house. She threw back the curtains to see a carpet of thick dew still lying in shady places on the ground.

Moving briskly in the fresh morning air, Meghan dressed in her tracksuit, joggers and scarf, judging it also wise to pull on her knitted woollen beanie for extra warmth, which effectively subdued her long red waves and the need to tie them back.

It was almost eight by the kitchen clock as she passed through and braved the crystal winter morning, gasping as its frosty fingers nipped at her few places of bare skin. She had hardly stepped out onto the back paved barbeque area open to the weak sun beneath the deciduous vine that would scramble overhead with lush greenery come spring, when she was joined by the family dogs snuffling excitedly around her legs.

'Hey, beautiful boys.' She heartily patted each one. 'You can show me the way.'

She did a few stretches then set off down a red dirt track away from the house, thick, high grasses glinting with dew drops on the verges.

★　★　★

As Dusty flung back the bedroom curtains, he stilled to discover Meghan emerging outside onto the patio. She wore exercise gear. Maybe she was into morning yoga or something. He almost felt a little guilty, like a voyeur, secretly spying on her as she raised her arms above her head, clasped her hands together and stretched side to side, limbering up. When she bent to touch her toes, he had a front row view of a rather pert backside.

She lifted each leg back in turn, bending it at the knee and holding the pose for a moment. After a few more exercises, he watched with fascination as she said something to the dogs, patted her leg, walked across the homestead lawn with the two family pets bounding joyfully around her ankles, and started jogging away from the house. Her red hair bobbed out behind her from underneath a snug woollen hat. So, she was a runner. Meghan Dorney was proving full of surprises.

His thoughts drifted. Alison had never taken the time for exercise. She had relied on a careful diet to maintain her trim figure. But then, she hadn't been the outdoor type anyway. Her days were absorbed at the computer or on the telephone working like a woman possessed to help market and promote the district and its farmers. Her professional efforts had almost immediately achieved results. He had been so proud of her, even if he occasionally resented their lack of time together.

Dusty snapped his focus back to the present. Meghan's image had grown smaller. He frowned, hoping she didn't get lost, and again considered his curiosity about this independent and cheerful newcomer to the district. A woman who would have a go. He turned away from the window to shower and dress. She'd be wanting a hot drink to thaw out when she returned.

Alison had appreciated the morning mug of tea he always brought to their bedroom of a weekend if she was home or on the rare days their lives coincided. In hindsight, those moments had been precious and brief. Along with the nostalgic thoughts was a deep accompanying guilt over her premature and tragic death. No one knew the truth and circumstances between them both leading up to that fateful night phone call to Sunday Plains from the police. And his long agonising drive in to Geraldton hospital on the coast, since Mallawa's medical centre wasn't equipped for serious life-threatening situations.

With a heavy sigh, he drowned his feeling of responsibility and remorse under a hot, stinging shower.

5

The sharp air quickened Meghan's footsteps, filling her with exhilaration to be a tiny speck in this vast landscape with not another soul in sight. It was so peaceful. Nutmeg and Clancy stuck with her.

Her face tingled with cold as she slowed her pace and then stopped. She turned in a complete circle. Nothing but grassy open plains. She vaguely glimpsed sheep off in the distance to the north. So *this* was what she had missed last night arriving in the dark. Paddocks with their first green flush of young wheat in endless seeded rows stretching away for miles.

'You guys are so lucky to live out here.' Meghan scratched Nutmeg's ears and was rewarded with a look of adoration. 'Well, the homestead's getting awfully small. Best be getting back, lads.'

As she approached the house again,

her heart swelled to see Dusty lounging against a patio post, only socks on his feet, ankles lazily crossed, a mug of steaming drink in one hand, the other sunk deep into the pocket of his jeans for warmth.

'Morning,' Meghan puffed, advancing across the damp lawn, removing her woollen hat and combing fingers through her mass of wavy hair.

'You're an early riser.' He regarded her softly.

She shrugged. 'Always have been.'

'You must be freezing.'

'It's pure Baltic, for sure, but invigorating. At least the dogs have had their exercise,' she chuckled.

Dusty pushed away from the post. 'Kettle's boiled. Coffee?'

'Tea. In a mug at least as big as yours.' She smiled.

The cosiness of indoors wrapped around her like a favourite blanket. As Dusty poured boiling water onto her teabag, Meghan removed her shoes, left them by the door and padded to the crackling fire. Dusty followed and handed her the drink. Their skin brushed as she accepted the mug. She cupped her cold hands around it to thaw out and backed up to the hearth.

'If you can spare half an hour this weekend, there's something I'd like to show you,' he said.

'Sure.' Meghan shrugged and was about to enquire further when Beth and Ollie emerged from the hallway.

'Morning, everyone,' his mother greeted. Ollie just grinned. 'How does fruit, pancakes and toast sound to you?' She addressed her son and grandson, ignoring Meghan, who tried not to be offended. Probably just the woman's usual manner. She withdrew from Dusty's quiet disarming presence, but he was soon besieged by his nephew anyway. Beth started gathering the makings for batter while Meghan, unasked but wanting to be helpful, chopped fruit, made toast and set the table.

'Everyone helps themselves,' Beth explained.

'I love the big kitchens you all have here and at Sunday Plains.' Meghan sighed, watching Beth pour dollops of batter onto the inbuilt griddle on the cooker.

As the batches cooked, Dusty crept to his mother's side and stole a pancake, slathering it with berry jam. 'Want one, champ?' he asked his nephew. Ollie nodded so he took another one, repeated the process and gave it to him.

Beth shook her head and grinned indulgently at her menfolk.

'Food.' Phil sauntered in, sniffing, Sally close behind.

'You know you'll be invited back, Meghan, if you keep making yourself so useful,' she quipped.

Meghan loved her sense of humour. 'I'm taking your kitchen back to my house in town,' she threatened. 'It's fabulous.'

'I need every inch of it during cropping and harvest. And when you're a long way from civilisation, people are always dropping in and staying.'

'It's rewarding cooking for a crowd, isn't it? My mother helps the chef in our pub. She prefers it to being behind the bar but she's taught me everything I know.'

Beth finished at the cooker and took the stack of pancakes to the table. Sally poured a mug of coffee and joined them.

'What family do you have, Meghan?' Beth asked, politely eating her syrupy pancakes.

She was surprised by her interest having previously been mostly ignored by the older woman. 'My parents, David and Aileen. Then I have an older brother, Kieran, who's married to Fiona, and they have my favourite two little terrors, Conor and Abby. Mum and Dad live above the pub but Kieran lives out of Rathdrum in a bungalow. He works in the pub, too, so it gives him some space away from working with the family all the time.'

Meghan felt Dusty's eyes constantly upon her from across the table. He had retrieved a box of cereal from under the island bench earlier, filling himself a bowl of wheat flakes, piling fruit on top and pouring over milk. Having demolished that, he was now working on a plateful of fruit and pancakes.

They lingered over cuppas until Sally pushed back her chair. 'Ready for some riding, Meghan?'

She nodded. 'Do I need to change?'

Sally shook her head. 'But you can borrow a pair of my boots. You coming, Ollie?'

'Yep.' He scrambled to his mother's side.

They left the homestead and strode across to the stables.

'This one's for you.' Sally patted a dun beauty with a white mane and blaze.

While Meghan saddled her horse, Sally led out her own bay mare and a small grey pony for Ollie. When they were all done, they trotted from the yards. The morning was gradually warming, with Meghan's mount eager and fit. She kept a light but firm grip on the rein as they followed the typical red dirt track away from the homestead.

After trotting in silence for a while, each absorbing the invigorating morning and settling into their ride, Sally called over, 'You're doing fine, Meghan. You don't look out of practice to me,' she teased. 'Up for a bit more pace?'

Meghan nodded.

'Keep up as best you can, Ollie,' she said, turning back to her son, who was trailing happily along behind. 'We'll head for the big dam, okay?'

He waved back, bouncing along happily on his pony. Meghan and Sally took off ahead.

Even beneath the weak wintry sun, Meghan hadn't felt so alive for ages. The open space and silence was awesome, its vast green beauty under young wheat crops, and the serenity refreshing. Meghan sighed with contentment.

They soon reached the dam and reined in. Sally turned around, grinning. 'Ollie's not far behind.' She dismounted and let the rein trail loose while the horses cropped the lush grasses. 'At dawn and dusk hundreds of birds flock here,' she said, hands on hips, gazing away across the dam.

'Must be a powerful sight.'

'And those small, dense, scrubby bushes with grey foliage all along the road are mulgas. We only see roos and emus further out in the grazing country. Do you know,' Sally added, her face lighting up with mischief, 'the whole United Kingdom would fit into Western Australia ten times over.'

'You're letting on.' Meghan's mouth dropped open in awe. 'It's huge out here. Clear to see from that first day I arrived.'

'I love the pink sunsets at the moment,' Sally said. She settled on the grass and Meghan joined her, hugging her knees. Ollie had quietly slid from his pony and was messing about down near the water with a stick. 'They turn fiery in summer,' she added. 'The colours are fabulous.'

'Crops are looking good.'

Sally nodded. 'We had early breaking rains this season just before you came, so it's promising for the harvest this year. Seeding can start as early as April or May if a cyclone dumps rain out here, or it can be as late as June or July. Every year is different. We usually employ seasonal workers in summer for the extra load. Give them accommodation and meals. I might be cooking for ten or fifteen people at dinner. Lunches I take out to them and we hire a local girl to help me.' She turned reflective and idly tugged blades of grass. 'I would have loved a daughter but I can't have any more children.'

'Oh, Sally.' Meghan's heart went out to her and she rested a hand gently on her arm.

She smiled faintly. 'I've accepted it now. I've had nothing but miscarriages since Ollie.' Her brow creased with disappointment. 'So he's probably destined to be our only little sparkling gem. I'm glad we were able to have a son for Phil and the future of the property. He's shaping up to be strong and silent like his Uncle Dusty,' she chuckled.

'Then he's going to become a remarkable man,' Meghan said without thinking.

Sally raised her eyebrows and grinned. 'Will he, now? And you know this from what, two meetings?'

Meghan shrugged off her gaffe. 'He's a top fella. Anyone can see that,' she defended quickly.

'You're right. And he has red dirt flowing in his veins.'

'I'm thinking it flows through all of you right down to little Ollie.'

Sally pushed a hand through her thick blonde hair and fondly contemplated her son. 'I guess we all do, at that. It's good to see Dusty smiling more these days, though we keep hinting he should pull back more. Stop working so hard. Take a break.'

'I gather it's taking time,' Meghan said quietly.

'Too long.' Sally shook her head. 'None of us deny Alison's death was an awful tragedy, but Dusty needs to move on.' She scowled and her gaze narrowed. 'There's something holding him back. Beth lost Daniel too soon, as well,' she went on. 'He was still a young man but she pushed forward and her life now is full. We don't forget those we love who are gone, but I've learned we grow from the pain of their passing. It strengthens our lives to have deeper purpose and meaning.'

Meghan drifted into reflection about the change in her own life without Dermot. After Sally's confidences and her easy trusting personality, she was tempted to share her own discontented circumstances but hesitated, feeling embarrassment at her own personal failure. Instead she said, 'You and Dusty have a sister.'

'Yes, our Sophie. She has a half share in a sheep station, Casuarina Downs, in the Flinders Ranges north of Adelaide in the South Australian outback. She's the oldest. She couldn't settle after Dad died. We were all close to him but she took his death especially hard. Over the last decade she's been travelling the world, working and saving. She came back to properties in the Northern Territory for experience, then did a stint in the iron ore mines up in the Pilbara.'

'Doing what, on earth?' Meghan asked.

'Management. She looks pretty darn cute in a hard hat. She's always been independent and set on having her own place one day. Her partner in the property at Casuarina Downs is a guy named Jack Bryce who she met while working in the mines. He was up there for the same reason. Make good money for a few years to help set himself up on a property too. They got talking and decided to join forces and get the land sooner.' She wrinkled up her nose. 'They've restored a beautiful old limestone homestead on the property. Don't think they're a couple though. Jack's too rustic. When Sophie meets a man he'll need to be a gentleman like our father and brother.' Sally squinted out across the dam. 'I admire my big sister so much, and we'd all love to see her settle down.'

'I'm sure she'll find the right one. We're all looking for someone special.'

They both sat in silence for a while until Sally said, 'Great place for meditation out here. I've done my share of thinking on this dam bank over the years.'

Ollie returned from playing and flung himself down onto the grass beside his mother. 'Look Mummy, an eagle.'

They all squinted skyward to watch the great bird wheeling overhead.

'I hope your father has the pizza oven fired up ready for lunch. Going to help me roll some dough when we get back?'

'Yep.' Ollie leapt up and giggled as he tried to pull his mother to her feet. Meghan rose to help and they mounted their horses still laughing, with bonds formed and new friendships made.

★　★　★

Ollie proved a young master at rolling pizza dough. 'You've done this before,' Meghan teased in the kitchen later.

'Yeah.'

When he flashed her his cheeky grin, her heart warmed. The quiet boy was coming around to her and she wasn't certain why that outcome was so important. Perhaps because Sally promised to become a good friend while she was here and this only child was so precious for his parents.

Beth and Meghan shared slicing and dicing vegetables, tomatoes, salami and olives, and grated mountains of cheese thickly layered over the toppings. It was awkward. The older woman didn't talk much and Meghan didn't want to push.

They took out trayfuls for Phil to slide into the oven. The big crunchy circles were cooked and crisp within minutes. The warmth from the brick dome kiln spread across the patio, so they ate the steaming slices with their fingers outdoors. Sally set a roll of paper towel on the table to rip off as needed and with the men drinking beer, the casual family meal and atmosphere reminded Meghan of Dorney gatherings back home. Nutmeg and Clancy stretched out near the oven, basking in its radiant heat.

'Phil's doing a barbeque tonight,' Sally announced.

'You're talking about dinner and we've barely finished lunch,' Meghan groaned.

'Don't be so cheeky. Your turn's coming.' Sally glanced across to Beth. 'Mum's making her legendary pot of vegetable soup tomorrow for lunch and you're on duty to produce one of your Guinness chocolate cakes.'

'You have Guinness?' Meghan queried.

'In the fridge as we speak.'

'So you only invited me out here to cook, then? The horses were just a decoy,' she laughed.

'Well, Ollie Barnes, you and I need to check over some school work and do your reader.' Sally rose and steered him indoors.

'And I'm taking a nap,' Beth sighed

and disappeared.

'That narrows down the company,' Phil chuckled.

Dusty sent a meaningful glance across to Meghan, who was nursing the lukewarm dregs of yet another huge mug of tea. 'You were up early jogging and riding horses. Do you need a rest, too, or can I steal that half hour now?'

She was intrigued and shrugged. 'I'm fine.'

As Dusty rose and they walked away, Meghan looked back over her shoulder. 'Phil, I'd say you've just volunteered for the dishes.'

'Are all Irish girls as saucy as you?' he drawled.

'No, and they're not half as much fun either,' she called out.

The dogs sensed adventure, stretched on their front paws and trotted after them. Meghan's awareness focused on Dusty. Walking at his side out to the sheds, he smelt of wood smoke and the breeze ruffled his hair. She didn't ask where they were going or why. Around this quiet man questions were unnecessary. She would find out soon enough.

'I hope you're not a woman who minds getting her hands dirty,' Dusty said above her thoughts.

'Now, if you'd seen me down in our pub cellar among kegs of beer, you wouldn't be asking me that question.'

He studied her for a moment then murmured, 'You're an interesting woman, Meghan Dorney.'

She almost wished he would ask if she had a boyfriend. Explain that, although still technically engaged, she was available. It seemed important he should know. It was early times between them but she couldn't ignore their simmering chemistry. Just being around him and hearing his name in conversation took her breath away. But with him living an hour from Mallawa, she understood the chances they would run into each other were likely to be slim.

They approached an open-fronted shed of farm and motor vehicles. Nutmeg disappeared but Clancy stayed close, sprawled out near his master, watchful.

'So are we going for a drive somewhere?' It couldn't be far. He said half an hour.

'Nope. Staying right here.' He pressed the remote on a medium-sized four-door sedan. 'This will suit our purpose nicely.' He reached in beside the driver's seat and popped the boot lever. 'Follow me.' Around the back he met her gaze and said, 'You're going to change a tyre.'

The penny dropped and Meghan grinned. 'Am I indeed?'

'Knowing how could save your life one day. While you're here,' he added casually.

'Okay, then.' Meghan rubbed her hands together. 'What's first?'

'For safety, make sure the hand brake is on.'

She checked inside the vehicle and pulled the lever.

Back at the rear of the car again, he said, 'The spare tyre should be in the boot under the floor mat.' His shoulder brushed against her as he leant forward to show her. The lesson was becoming more interesting by the minute, but it was most distracting having him so close. She'd best concentrate or she'd not remember a word he said. As he pointed out, this was important.

'See this screw here?' She nodded. 'There's usually one that secures the spare tyre and all the necessary bits. Undo it.'

She did, which revealed the tyre underneath, the lifting jack to raise the car and a wheel spanner to loosen the nuts. He helped her manhandle the spare onto the ground, then disappeared for a moment. Clancy nosed closer, curious.

'Hey, boy,' she chuckled, rubbing his ears. 'You going to help me?'

Dusty returned with the car owner's manual. 'This usually shows you where to place the jack to lift the car. Depending on which wheel, of course.' He handed her the spanner. 'This is where you'll need some elbow grease.'

His deep voice was so soft and companionable beside her. Meghan thought, *Oh I'll be needing a lot more than that*. One by one, she forced the wheel nuts loose, mostly by standing on it and pushing hard with her foot.

'Leave the nuts on but loose. Now we need to put the jack in place.'

Next thing, Meghan was kneeling on the ground getting dirty setting up the jack and winding the handle like mad until the tyre was just high enough off the ground to remove.

When that was done, she grinned at him foolishly. 'This'll be taking me more like an hour.' Not that she minded. It meant longer in his company.

'It's your first time. You're doing fine.'

Meghan was childishly cheered to hear it. When was the last time Dermot had given her a compliment or any sign of encouragement?

'You okay?' Dusty asked quietly, sitting on his haunches beside her, hands folded between his knees. Clancy hovered and nuzzled him.

'Fine.' She hesitated. 'I appreciate you doing this.'

'You're welcome,' he murmured.

It became such a charged and intimate moment, Meghan was tempted to lean forward and plant a kiss on that appealing mouth but felt a traitor for even thinking such a thing. And her an engaged woman. Instead she asked, 'What's next?'

'You need to take off the wheel nuts now and try to jiggle the wheel off. And be careful.' A gentle note of caution entered his voice. 'It will be heavy.'

She kept following Dusty's warmly voiced easy instructions, removing the tyre onto the ground and insisting she place it under the car.

'Why?'

He met her gaze. 'In case the jack fails or sinks in loose dirt. The tyre will support the car. It could save a life or limb, so don't ever get under a car while its jacked up, okay?'

Meghan nodded. Beyond caution, there was also heartfelt concern in his command.

'Sure. Put the spare on now, then?'

'Think you can handle it on your own?'

She could have played the helpless female but that wasn't her style. 'I'll give it a shot.' She grunted and struggled to line it up, letting out a small whoop of delight when she managed to get it on. Presuming she reversed the whole process now, she began replacing and tightening the wheel nuts. When she was done, Dusty helped her pull the tyre out from under the car and wind down the jack.

With everything stowed back in its rightful place in the boot, he handed her a rag. It looked like a man's old checked shirt cut up for the purpose. She wiped her hands thoroughly, then planted them on her hips to admire her work. 'I can't believe I just did that.'

'I admire anyone who has a go.'

'Never let it be said,' she chuckled. 'Thanks for the lesson. Not as daunting as I thought. You'd make a good teacher,' she observed. 'You have patience and Lord knows you need plenty of that in

117

the classroom,' she quipped.

'Where did you two both disappear to?' Beth challenged sharply the moment they stepped in the back door of the homestead again.

Meghan reeled at the suspicious note in her voice. Phil, Sally and Ollie, chattering in the living room by the fire, all flashed a questioning glance in their direction. Everyone fell silent.

Dusty glowered. 'I showed Meghan how to change a tyre. She's vulnerable out here. It was equally important for Alison, too, on more than one occasion. I believe it was one of the first things Dad taught you, wasn't it?'

'Yes, of course,' Beth said quietly, corrected.

Deciding it best to help lighten the atmosphere, Meghan punched the air with her fist. 'I am now Mallawa's newest tyre changer.'

Although everyone laughed and good-natured banter followed, an air of tension still floated around. Meghan judged it wise to take a break from the family and give them some space. 'Well, I'm officially grimy.' She glanced down at her grease-stained clothes. 'I'd best go clean up and change.'

And in her lovely guest room, Meghan took her time about it. She had been in her tracksuit all day. After a long hot shower, she stepped out and pulled on a clean pair of jeans and black knitted sweater, brushing the tangles from her tawny waves. She tamed her hair with a clasp and when she reappeared in the kitchen later, Ollie was perched on a stool crunching on carrot sticks while Sally prepared salads. Beth was nowhere to be seen but through the panoramic kitchen windows, Phil and Dusty were out on the patio barbequing meat and onions.

'Feeling refreshed?' Sally asked, glancing up from her task.

Meghan nodded. 'After scuttling around in dirt, I felt like a right grub.'

'Wine?'

'Please. Can I help?'

'No. Nearly done. Ollie,' she said

brightly, 'want to go out and see how the steaks and sausages are going?' He slid off the chair. 'And best feed the dogs while you're out there, okay?'

'Yeah.'

When her son was outside, Sally glanced to the bedroom wing doorway and lowered her voice. 'I apologise for Mum being a bit sharp earlier. I can't understand what got into her.'

'Have I offended her in some way?'

Sally shook her head. 'Heavens, no. You're fun and easygoing and you've fitted in this weekend as though we've been friends for years.' She reached over and laid her hand on Meghan's. 'Thanks for that. It's lovely to have someone my own age that I can connect with.'

'I've loved every moment,' Meghan assured her. 'And I appreciate your invitation.'

Sally hesitated as she dressed the salad, tossing in a handful of chopped herbs. 'Mum worried me today,' she confided. 'You know, for the first time since Alison died, she's being controlling about Dusty.'

'Not surprising,' Meghan said generously.

'Perhaps, but I think Mum can see that for the first time since Ally's gone, Dusty's enjoying another woman's company. He's never let himself do that until now.'

'Dusty's just a good friend, Sally. Nothing more.'

'Maybe,' she hedged, giving the impression she considered Meghan's protest open to doubt.

Before Meghan could respond, Ollie burst back into the kitchen. 'Dad said the food's ready.'

'Great timing. So are the salads.'

At that moment, too, Beth wandered in from her room, so their chat was interrupted.

'Mum and Meghan,' Sally said, 'if you could each take out a bowl of salad, I'll bring the wine.'

Guarded now, especially since Beth's reappearance, Meghan deliberately sat away from Dusty, tuning in to the general conversation among the family but keeping her head down and eating her meal in silence, pretending Beth's slight didn't matter. It did. She admired the older woman. She was independent and a respected district icon. So her acceptance of Meghan was important, and it troubled her because she didn't have it. She knew the cause. Protecting her son. But Meghan felt she was overdoing it.

The genuine feelings brewing between herself and Dusty justified exploration but, after the tragic loss of his wife, any approach must come from him first. She sighed. Was this too soon to be interested in another man while Dermot still hovered on the fringes of her life back in Ireland? She had never factored in any such possibility when she'd left home for six months.

Much later after the barbeque, when Ollie's protests about bed time were overcome, Phil turned the stereo to some easy listening music and pulled Sally up to dance. She peeked around her husband's shoulder. 'Dusty, it's no fun being a wallflower. Ask Meghan to dance,' she urged playfully.

Beth glowered at her daughter's suggestion. Dusty either didn't see the disapproval or chose to ignore it, for he lifted his eyebrows slightly in query.

Meghan smiled and shrugged. 'I could teach you an Irish reel,' she joked.

Dusty moved toward her and held out his hand. 'Maybe another time.'

She drifted into his arms with such ease, relishing his warmth against her. Dusty conveyed an unleashed energy as though holding himself back. As she was, too. In the name of decorum in front of the family, she kept her feelings in check and her mood light as they danced.

When an older melody took its place, Meghan reluctantly pulled away and glanced at Beth. 'This sounds like one your mother would enjoy.' Beth preened at the gesture and, as Meghan stepped aside, Dusty drew his mother to her feet.

Meghan watched the dynamics in the room. Beth gracious and doting on her son. Phil and Sally murmuring and smiling intimately, clearly still very much in love. A couple in tune with each other and meant to be together. Which clearly contrasted her own lack of any such deep feelings for Dermot.

Meghan fingered her left hand where his ring used to be. The tedium of fulfilling his lifestyle, dressing up, perfectly groomed and smiling, making social banter, had worn thin. The widening the gulf with Dermot only marked their differences and the end of their weakening relationship.

Meghan's thoughts were interrupted when Ollie toddled into the room, sleepily rubbing his eyes. 'What's the matter, Ollie?' Meghan hunkered down to his level and held his hands.

'I woke up because of the music.'

'Did you have your bedroom door shut?' she asked gently. He shook his head. She smiled. 'Maybe it was that, then?' She wrinkled her nose and lowered her voice in confidence. 'How about we leave your mum and dad to keep dancing. Is it all right if I take you back to bed instead and we'll close your door?'

Ollie nodded. By then his small warm hand had found hers and they were heading back along the bedroom wing hallway. With Ollie tucked into bed again and the doona pulled up to his chin, Meghan kissed him lightly on the forehead.

'Sleep tight, Ollie,' she murmured.

'Are we going riding again tomorrow?' he yawned.

'I hope so. And I'm making a wicked chocolate cake,' she whispered, 'So I might need a hand with the mixing and tasting.' He barely nodded in response. Meghan rose from the bed. 'I'll close all the doors after me so the music's not so loud, okay?' But the boy was already rolling over and closing his eyes.

Back in the living room as the music ended, Sally asked, 'Everything all right?'

Meghan nodded. 'Music was a bit loud so I closed all the doors.'

'Thanks. He normally sleeps through anything. Want a cuppa or a nightcap?'

'No, thank you. I'll turn in.' They hugged. 'Thanks for everything today. It's been grand.'

'Our pleasure.'

'Night all.'

Meghan's glance included everyone. She didn't look back but felt the warmth of Dusty's gaze on her as she left the room. A short time later, snuggled cosily in bed and feeling dozy, she heard his movements next door and found comfort in them.

6

After her early-morning run in the opposite direction next day, Meghan returned to the homestead hoping to see Dusty but found Sally propped against the counter sipping her first coffee of the day.

'I didn't wake you, did I?'

Sally shook her head and groaned. 'Phil was snoring. Only does it when he's really relaxed. Great night, wasn't it?'

Meghan grinned. 'Lovely.'

'We'll be having Sunday brunch later so if you can hold out for food for an hour or so, we could get in another ride,' Sally said hopefully.

'Absolutely.'

'You've no idea how I appreciate you giving up your weekend and coming all the way out here. I'm so enjoying your company.'

'Me, too.'

They grinned, realised they were having a girlie moment and smacked hands in a high five. Laughter greeted Ollie when he appeared fully dressed seconds later.

Sally raised her eyebrows. 'Morning, young man. And what are your plans?'

His face briefly fell. 'Aren't we going riding?' His mother nodded and he beamed. 'Is Miss Dorney coming?'

'Yes.'

Meghan tilted her head and glanced at Sally. 'If your mother says it's okay, how about at your house you call me Meghan?'

Listening in, Sally added, 'But at school you'll need to remember it's Miss Dorney.'

His blond head nodded vigorously and his eyes sparkled to be part of a special confidence.

'Want a hot chocolate before we go?' Sally asked them.

'Nope,' they replied in unison.

'Let's head out then.'

This morning, Sally led them away across unfenced grassy countryside lush with winter green. They stopped for a while to let the horses rest and graze, then headed back for the homestead. Halfway home, they met Phil and Dusty with Beth in the back seat of a twin cab utility. Dusty smiled at her and lifted his big hat but didn't say a word. From the back seat, Beth witnessed the exchange and glowered.

Phil leaned out the window. 'Just heading off around the sheep.'

'Haven't forgotten brunch?' Sally teased.

He chuckled. 'Beth's soup's simmering, damper's ready to go in the oven, so we just need that evil chocolate cake Meghan promised.'

She laughed. 'I'm on it as soon as we get back.'

Phil put the utility into gear and drove off.

'Mum was quiet this morning,' Sally said as they rode home.

'Do you think she'll brighten up if I

stay away from your brother?'

Meghan was serious but Sally blazed back, 'Don't you dare! You're good for him. It's been too long since he unwound and spent a weekend with us.' Stalling any further argument, she challenged, 'Race you back,' but had urged her mare into a gallop before Meghan even heard the dare. All the same, she gave her friend a run for her money and Ollie pulled up close behind.

Back in the homestead kitchen, the aroma of Beth's bubbling pot of thick vegetable soup greeted them. Sally put the damper in the oven and brewed them all rich milky mugs of hot chocolate, dropping two marshmallows in each. Meanwhile, Meghan called out the ingredients for her chocolate cake and Ollie collected them from the huge walk-in pantry.

'Seems a pity to use Guinness in a cake,' Meghan quipped as she opened the can of dark beer. 'All the old fellas at the bar back home would say it's a waste of a fine drop.'

Ollie hovered while Meghan heated the Guinness and butter together, then she let him break off and drop in pieces of dark chocolate while she stirred in the sugar. After the mixture cooled, Meghan stirred in sour cream and flour while Ollie cracked in the eggs. The batter was barely mixed when he scooped his finger in for a taste.

'Ollie Barnes, I hope that hand is clean,' his mother scolded, pretending to look fierce.

Ollie chuckled. 'I already washed 'em.'

'Does it pass the test?' Meghan asked. Ollie nodded furiously because his mouth was too full to speak. 'Right, into the cooker then and we'll whip up some cream.'

Then the others returned and once more it was everyone around the long table to enjoy Beth's thick soup and slices of warm damper. There was an awkward moment as they all took their seats when Dusty pulled out a chair beside Meghan. She didn't dare glance toward Beth at the head of the table to catch her reaction.

Everyone took a break between courses until Meghan sliced her dessert cake into generous portions with a dollop of cream and they all clambered around the table again. Few words were spoken as they devoured it.

Phil clattered his fork onto an empty plate and said to Meghan, 'I hope you're leaving this recipe with Sally.'

'After your hospitality this weekend, it's the least I can do.'

'Guinness and chocolate. What's not to like?' Dusty murmured beside her so softly Meghan almost didn't catch his light-hearted quip.

Replete, they all lounged around the fire after brunch. Beth and Ollie played board games but, as the day passed, a veil of reflection settled over them, knowing the town visitors must soon leave. Meghan wondered if Sally deliberately kept herself busy making thick ploughman's sandwiches for the four travellers' return journey to divert her attention from yet another parting from her son.

'We phone him every night,' Sally confided when Meghan came over to help wrap the sandwich bundles. 'But we still miss him dreadfully. One of the few snags of living in the outback.' She gave a wistful smile. 'He'll be off to private college in Perth when he's older but I'm ignoring that fact at the moment,' she admitted.

'I can imagine it must be difficult.'

When the bags were packed and it came time for goodbyes, Meghan was torn to be leaving but cheered by her new friendship with Sally. She eyed Beth cautiously. The jury was yet to cast its vote on that one just because Dusty had shown more than a passing interest in her. Meghan puzzled why Beth wasn't happier for him and his tentative recovery from his wife's untimely death.

Sally hugged Meghan warmly. 'We'll keep in touch even after you go back to Ireland.'

'That time is a long way off yet and doesn't bear thinking about. I plan to enjoy my time here while I can.'

As they all moved amongst each other hugging and saying farewells, Meghan caught the wistful sadness on Dusty's face. She figured it was because he was leaving his sister's family.

It was too obvious when Beth hopped up into the front seat of her vehicle next to Dusty. Meghan grinned to herself but happily sat in the back with Ollie. With all arms waving madly, they finally sped away.

Ollie started his ploughman's sandwich soon after leaving. Between munching on his picnic dinner, gazing out the window and playing his Game Boy, he seemed happy enough to be heading back into Mallawa for another school week with his grandmother. Conversation dwindled between Dusty and Beth as the sun set and they approached Sunday Plains again.

Ollie waved his uncle goodbye but stayed in the four-wheel drive playing his games. Dusty stepped out and retrieved his bag from the rear while Beth briefly disappeared indoors, leaving Meghan and Dusty alone together.

He dropped his bag in the dust, reached out and squeezed her hand. 'Take care.'

She nodded, suddenly tongue-tied. 'You, too.' On a mischievous impulse, she said, 'Bring yourself into town some time and I'll repay your hospitality.'

Her comment seemed to tip the balance of his indecision, because those brown eyes grew warmer, he gave her a tug and pulled her against him, lowering his head to give her a resounding goodbye kiss.

Stunned, Meghan thought *Dammit* and made it last. It would be weeks before she saw him again. So she kissed him back. Good and proper.

'You're a bold fella,' she breathed afterwards.

'I think we both enjoyed it,' he murmured.

'To be sure. You're a dark horse full

of surprises, aren't you now?'

This was definitely a moment. But their intimacy was short-lived and spoiled when Beth emerged from the house and Meghan caught her shocked glance over Dusty's shoulder. She must have seen them from the house! This was ridiculous. An adult feeling guilty because they'd kissed.

He turned at his mother's approach and enveloped her in a farewell hug which Meghan thought she returned rather stiffly.

As Beth headed for her vehicle, Meghan cleared her throat and offered, 'I'm happy to drive. If you're feeling tired.'

'I'm perfectly fine and capable, thank you,' she snapped.

Taken aback by the short response, Meghan climbed into the front passenger seat, closed her eyes and pretended to doze for most of the one-hour drive back into Mallawa, but her mind reeled with thoughts of Dusty.

So this was how it felt to be attracted

again. She'd forgotten. Long ago she had experienced lesser feelings for Dermot. Once, she had thought he was *the one*, but now knew she was mistaken. Her body filled with a far greater heat for Dusty that only increased whenever they met. But she pulled back warily. What if this, too, in time was a mistake? How would she know?

She must learn to cope with this new searing attraction for a man all over again. Nothing was resolved in her life back in Ireland, so she must tread softly. For Dusty's sake as much as her own. To see if deeper and lasting feelings developed. Meanwhile, she would let him lead wherever their unfolding friendship was destined to go. But it sure felt right at the moment.

Beth left the engine running when she dropped off Meghan at her house, clearly anxious to leave. Ollie was asleep in the back so she said a hasty good night.

★ ★ ★

In the following weeks, Meghan was kept busy and given no time to dwell on her personal life. Because she was a compassionate and experienced teacher who learned as much from her students as they did from her, she thrived on working with individual students. When she mentioned to Barbara the subtle distinctions she had noticed between teaching the white and Aboriginal children, an enlightening discussion followed.

'For the first five years, those children are immersed with their parents. They don't come from an environment where reading, writing and maths are part of everyday life.' Meghan listened with interest as Barbara spoke. 'At home, an Aboriginal child waits to be told. If they question or pester adults, they might be considered cheeky.'

'Really?' Meghan was surprised.

Barbara nodded. 'So it's vital to understand their background because in a normal classroom situation, a child who is outgoing and asks questions is praised and rewarded.'

'So any student who doesn't might be considered lazy or slow?' Meghan offered.

'Exactly.' Barbara smiled. 'That's why I wanted to give you the opportunity while you're here to connect with *all* our students. There's such a vast integration of all cultures in the world today, learning to appreciate them can only benefit your teaching skills. The difference between coping and failing can be as simple as understanding.'

'I agree.'

Although on their Skype interview and chats Barbara had roughly outlined what she might encounter differently here, she had mainly thought this temporary outback teaching experience simply meant living and working in a remote Australian town. With Barbara's explanations about local customs in the community, her insight grew.

'Aboriginal parents watch their children but don't necessarily punish them for wrongs. They are just expected to get it right next time.' Barbara grinned.

'Makes sense.'

'They're allowed to learn at their own pace and are encouraged to develop observational skills. If a child doesn't look directly at you, he might consider it disrespectful and, as their teacher, you might consider the student shy.'

Meghan had arrived in Mallawa toward the end of the first school semester to give her time to assimilate and settle into the school and community for the second half of the year, which she now considered she had well and truly done.

As the holidays approached, Meghan knew she would have some free time. Although willingly drawn into NAIDOC preparations and events for one week, the other one loomed aimlessly ahead.

It felt like forever since her weekend out at Bindi station. Sally had phoned for chats a few times but to her disappointment, she heard nothing from Dusty. She wasn't a woman to sit and pine but, frankly, based on their cracker of a first kiss, she would have loved to hear from him again. He'd certainly made an unforgettable impression. Every time her phone rang, she always hoped it was from Sunday Plains. Maybe her growing feelings weren't mutual after all?

For NAIDOC week, her friend Carrie Edwards was designated events photographer and was seen every spare moment with her camera equipment set up and aimed at students and locals alike, both in the school grounds and around Mallawa. Although the Aboriginal flag always flew at the school beside the Australian one, there was a special symbolic flag-raising ceremony to mark the first day of celebrations.

Each day there was another event organised. First up were traditional native body-painting and didgeridoo lessons, with the Aboriginal children leading the classes. It made for much fun and laughter, not to mention an appreciation of expertise. Try as she might, Meghan could not get any sound out of the long painted hollow timber wind instrument that even small children, especially the boys, made look so easy. She loved its deep haunting and rhythmic sound.

The second day was a major event involving the whole community and held in the broad main street of town, closed off to traffic for the festivities. After escorting the children with the other teachers from the school where they had roles in music performances or duties as food-stall holders, everyone was free to go their own way and enjoy the day.

Meghan's heart tumbled with pleasure to spy the welcome familiar sight of Dusty in the crowd. When he caught sight of her from a distance, his big hat partly shading those warm brown eyes she remembered so well, his mouth tilted into a grin. Like magnets, they were drawn toward each other.

'Meghan. Nice to see you again,' he drawled.

Nice? Well, if he was playing it cool, so could she. 'You're a stranger in town.

Sure you haven't lost your way now?'

'Demands of sheep,' he explained. He held her gaze, looking genuinely unsure. His embarrassment was endearing. 'About the other weekend.' He looked down and kicked a boot in the dirt. 'I shouldn't have taken advantage.'

Meghan's spirits slumped. Was he warning her off? Regretting he'd made an advance? After all, she was only a temporary Mallawa resident, and he didn't share his emotions easily since Alison's loss.

'Fair enough,' she said quietly and waited for his next move.

'Are you free for a while?'

She shrugged. 'All day, really.'

They sauntered through the stalls and festivities together, hit by wonderful aromas from food tents as they passed. Finally they succumbed and tasted the kangaroo stew. Meghan was hesitant, but Dusty assured her their huge mob numbers were allowed to be officially culled. The meat was strong and tasty and Meghan mopped up the remaining juices with her slice of damper.

When Dusty wandered away from the crowds, Meghan followed. He led her to a gazebo in the central garden strip that divided each side of the main street. He removed his broad hat and rested it on the bench alongside. Seated close together with the mild winter sunshine on their backs and the distant movement and hum of the crowds in the background, Meghan found it impossible to remain detached in his distracting company.

'The children have been explaining the purpose of NAIDOC week to me. It's a wonderful tradition.'

Dusty nodded. 'Helps the rest of us understand our country's first people better. Like many things, it came out of discontent and protest.'

'How did it start?'

Dusty stretched out an arm behind her. It was a casual gesture, natural because of his long limbs. Meghan closed her eyes to soak up the moment and the deep soothing sound of his voice.

'Unrest about the treatment of the Aborigines. Reached a turning point just before the Second World War. Protesters marched through Sydney on Australia Day.' He glanced down at her to explain. 'January the twenty-sixth, when we celebrate our country's founding. Like your St. Patrick's Day, I guess, when you celebrate Ireland's heritage and culture.'

'Oh,' she murmured, understanding.

'A deputation to our prime minister proposed a national policy for our Aboriginal people, but sadly it was rejected. For years they continued an annual Day of Mourning on the Sunday before Australia Day, then decided to change it from a protest day to celebrating Aboriginal culture instead.'

'It's a grand idea. Especially if it brings visitors into town,' she teased, turning her face toward him. For a fraction of a second he started to lean forward. Meghan hoped he might kiss her again but he changed his mind and straightened.

Dusty cleared his throat. 'Up for more food and entertainment?' he said, rising and settling his big hat comfortably on his head again. 'Quandongs and ice cream?'

'I've heard the children talking about them. Some kind of bush food, isn't it?'

Dusty nodded and led her back onto the street. 'Edible fruit off the desert sandalwood tree. It's used for jams and chutneys and has medicinal uses too.'

Meghan felt alive in Dusty's company but hid it well. She tried to ignore if any part of him accidentally brushed against her as he led her through the crowds. Dermot would never take time off for a day like this.

After lunch, Sally, Phil and Ollie's happy faces emerged from the crowd.

'Hey, champ,' Dusty greeted his nephew, giving his trademark rustling of the lad's mop of hair.

The men shook hands and the women hugged, then Dusty kissed his sister on the cheek. They quickly caught up on news, then all walked to the recreation oval where the crowd gathered and took up seats to watch a special afternoon musical performance.

Meghan's mood lifted with Dusty beside her and she proudly witnessed the children she had coached, both Aboriginal and white, joining together to dazzle their community with colourful presentations and items of traditional dance and a corroboree, ending with a massed choir of stirring harmonies.

With whistles of appreciation and resounding applause that left their hands aching, everyone wandered back to the main street. Some groups of males adjourned to the pub, families had picnics and barbeques in the central gardens, and food-stall tents still operated on the street.

'You coming around to Mum's for dinner, Dusty?' Sally asked.

He sank his hands into his pockets and said casually, 'I'll be along shortly. I'll walk Meghan home.'

'Sure.' Sally glanced between them with interest.

Everyone hugged and they parted.

'If you're meant to be with family,'

Meghan said, 'I can walk home by myself, you know. It's not dark yet and I do know the way.'

'They won't mind.'

Meghan wasn't so sure. Frowning, she jumped in, 'If your mother is expecting — '

'She can wait. She'll understand.'

Meghan doubted it when Beth discovered who had made her son late. Dusty sank his hands into his pockets and turned in the direction of her house. She couldn't deny enjoying his warm protective company and welcomed it a while longer. He would disappear out to Sunday Plains again soon enough.

Still, Meghan grew uncertain when she and Dusty finally reached her place. There was a tense, awkward moment when she speculated if Dusty would kiss her again. But her longing proved unnecessary when she realised someone was sitting on her back doorstep in the dusk.

'Hi, Meggie. You've sure taken your time.'

7

'Claire Murphy!'

Meghan gaped while a thousand questions crammed her mind at the unexpected sight of her brunette Irish friend and the large suitcase beside her. Claire leapt to her feet and they hugged.

Meghan suffered a moment's alarm and pulled back. 'Nothing's wrong back home, is there?'

'No, no. Nothing like that.' Claire peered over her shoulder.

Meghan half turned. 'Dusty, this is my best friend in all the world.'

'When we're not bickering,' Claire chuckled.

Meghan smiled. 'True. Claire Murphy, Dusty Nash,' she introduced them. 'Dusty has a property out of town and his sister, Sally, is a good friend, too.'

Meghan played her cards casually, hoping Claire didn't read more into her arrival home in the twilight with a drop-dead handsome fella while she was still engaged to someone else back home.

Dusty moved forward and extended a hand. 'A pleasure.'

Claire preened, stroked a hand over her hips and beamed. 'It most certainly is.' She grasped his hand for longer than Meghan felt necessary.

'Welcome to Mallawa,' Dusty drawled.

Claire cast a narrowed, sharp-eyed gaze over Meghan and Dusty. 'So you've been on a date then?'

'No,' Dusty jumped in swiftly. Meghan felt deflated but grateful for the rescue. 'It's been an Aboriginal celebration day in town. Just seeing Meghan home safely before dinner with my family.'

Claire seemed satisfied for the moment but Meghan knew her nosy friend wouldn't resist asking more tricky questions.

'I'll let you two ladies catch up,' Dusty saved her again as he took his leave. 'Nice meeting you, Claire.'

'Likewise.'

'Night, Meghan,' he said softly and sent her a meaningful glance. With a canny grasp of character and situation, he had turned cautious. Meghan wanted to hug him in relief. If Claire suspected she was interested in any man other than Dermot, the embarrassment and explosion didn't bear thinking about.

No one out here knew she was engaged and Dusty might think her fickle. It would look like she was eyeing him up and leading him on while her fiancé was thousands of miles away in Ireland. Until now, there seemed no point in telling anyone. Yet. Until it was official. Come December and her return to Ireland, Dermot would no longer be part of her life.

As Dusty strode away, Meghan felt a pang of disappointment to be deprived of a few more precious moments in his company. But she planted a broad smile on her face as she unlocked her back door.

'Come on in. You're lucky I've a spare bedroom, otherwise you might have to grab a room at the pub.'

She tried to hide her annoyance when Claire's sudden appearance should have been a wonderful surprise. For once, against her feelings, she hoped Dusty stayed out at Sunday Plains so there was no chance of Claire picking up on any signals Meghan's body language betrayed when around him. It was difficult to hide sparks you felt but were forced to deny.

Claire hauled her suitcase up the step and into the kitchen.

'So what made you decide to visit? You're a city girl. I thought outback Australia would be the last place you'd come,' Meghan quipped as she threw open the windows to invite the warm early spring evening air indoors.

Claire gave a casual shrug. 'Is that what you hoped?'

Meghan spun around on alert. 'Excuse me?'

Claire nodded toward the door. 'Is that gorgeous fella your secret fling while poor Dermot's on the other side of the world?'

Meghan stared at her friend, speechless. The accusation had come out of nowhere with Claire barely five minutes in the house, but it was so close to the truth . . .

'You know me better than that,' she said quietly. A stab of guilt darted through her. Truthfully, she *was* attracted to Dusty, no denying that, and they *had* kissed. With Claire's arrival and innocent allegation, Meghan now felt like the biggest heel for even looking at another man.

'Dusty's just one of many friends I've made here in recent months.'

'So, is this Sally your new best friend instead of me then?'

'Oh, jaysus.' Meghan laughed. 'You're five minutes in the door and at it already.'

'What!' Claire pouted, trying to look cute and innocent.

Meghan was wise to her wiles but men fell for them all the time. 'Being jealous,' she pointed out in exasperation. 'You have other friends besides me and I don't mind.' When Claire gave a genuine yawn, Meghan added tactfully,

'Let's not go there tonight, eh? You've had a long flight.'

'You're telling me. It took me a whole bloody day just sittin' on me backside on a plane to get here.'

Meghan wondered why she had — especially without letting on that she was coming — but pushed that conversation aside for later. Instead, she dragged Claire's weighty suitcase toward the hallway.

'Follow me. You can freshen up while I open a bottle of wine then we can have a chinwag.'

When Claire emerged half an hour later, her heavy makeup refreshed, hair fluffed, long legs in tight jeans, her feet in heels and a white lacy blouse fitted to her shapely body, Meghan almost dropped the glass of wine she handed across to her. 'Are you planning on going out?'

'I saw a pub as we drove in. Any chance of action?'

Meghan sighed. Claire the party girl. 'In a small outback town?' She grinned. 'Not really.' She paused. 'So, how did you get out here to town, then?'

'To be honest with you, I thumbed it.'

'Claire!' Meghan scolded gently.

Most people were trustworthy and usually only tourists or locals headed out to Mallawa. Still, Claire had taken a risk and it paid to be careful. There were always roughnecks out there.

'Well I'm glad you arrived safely. Who gave you a lift?'

Claire shrugged. 'Some fella going out to a mine further on with a weird long name.'

Meghan grinned. 'Koolanooka. Iron ore.'

Claire took a long taste of her wine. 'His name was Sam and he was cute in a rugged kind of way. Sort of a rough diamond, if you get my meaning.' She winked.

Meghan shook her head. If Claire was more than a five-minute walk from a dress boutique and a cafe strip, she'd shrivel up and die. She spent most weekends in Dublin shopping. She would never seriously consider a rugged outdoor type, but she did love to flirt.

'I'm flattered you managed the air fare just for me,' Meghan hinted. Claire's credit cards always smoked from overuse and she looked forward to the explanation.

'Well, now, there's a story for you. I was half langered at the pub a few weeks back when your fiancé walks in. I was moaning about you being gone. Then and there he says to me, 'Claire, you should go and pay your best friend a visit,' and offered to pay for my ticket.'

They eyed each other from where they had moved into the lounge and settled into comfy chairs. Meghan gaped, wondering why he hadn't come himself but sent Claire instead.

'Dermot?' She gulped back her astonishment and confusion.

Dermot O'Brien never did anything for someone else unless there was something in it for him personally. What benefit did he gain by Claire coming out here? All this way? To such an isolated place? When he knew Claire's sociable urban personality as well as she? Meghan's suspicions were instantly triggered. To spy?

'That was right generous of him. He didn't suggest coming out himself then?' Meghan said wryly.

'Oh, you know Dermy.' Claire waved her glass of wine in the air. 'It's all about work.'

Dermy?

'Now there's a man who'll take care of his woman,' she pointed out almost sadly before drinking the last of her wine and holding it out for another.

Depends what the woman wants or needs, Meghan thought. 'Well I'm pleased you made the effort. It's grand to see a face from home.'

'You must miss him then.' Claire leaned forward as Meghan refilled her glass. 'Dermot.'

Meghan hedged, then decided it might be nice to unburden herself of the truth. She'd already hinted her waning feelings to her mother before

157

she left, so it couldn't hurt to mention it to her best friend.

'To be honest with you Claire, not as much as I expected.'

Claire gaped while processing the implication. 'You do still love him though, don't you?' She sounded more hopeful than concerned.

'I'm not sure.'

'Meggie Dorney! What are you saying?'

'I'm saying I accepted this job to take time out and think.'

'About Dermy? What's not to like?' she scoffed.

Meghan felt a jolt of intuition. What had been going on back home in Ireland while she was away?

'I'm not sure Dermot is for me after all, Claire. Like you said, he's all about work and ambition. Family and kids are way down his list.'

'How do you know?'

'I asked him after we were engaged, trying to get a handle on our future together.'

'What did he say?'

'After a few years. Maybe.' Meghan paused and contemplated her friend, eyes wide, cheeks flushed. From the wine or the direction of the conversation? 'I love kids, Claire. You know that. I teach them all day and want a brood of my own.'

'For sure. It's always been that way with you. You're always doting on Conor and Abby.'

'I wish my brother would have more,' Meghan laughed. 'But Fiona's content with two.' Talking of family back home had turned her wistful.

Claire grew serious too. 'So does Dermot know your feelings, then?'

'We didn't discuss them before I left. He's probably barely aware I'm missing,' she said with heartfelt bitterness. 'If he really loved me to bits more than anything else in the world, I would have heard from him often, but he's barely made contact. He sends me an occasional email but my time away out here was as much a test for him as it was for me. He failed, Claire.' Meghan pulled a rueful grin. 'If he still wanted me, I'd know it.'

At least Claire had the grace to look awkward even as Meghan suspected what might have begun to develop since she was away. She was surprised but not bothered. In her heart, she knew her engagement to Dermot was over. Face to face on her return to Ireland, she'd make it official, but doubted he would raise any objections or beg her to reconsider. Glancing across at a flushed Claire, Meghan realised how far Ireland and Dermot had been pushed to the back reaches of her mind.

'I'm sorry to hear that, Meggie. Really I am. But I have to say in his defence, Dermot's a man going places. You'd be mad not to think on it some more.'

'Exactly what I've been doing these past months. But what if I don't want the world he's offering, Claire, or a man who puts me second? What if I just want a man who'll simply love me for life?'

Claire raised her dark kohl eyebrows in amazement and Meghan suspected she had no idea what she was talking about. Her friend would love a fella one day, too, but she would happily be a doormat for him, something Meghan would never be prepared to do. She wanted a marriage with equality and respect, like her own parents'.

'If that kind of fella works for you, Claire, you're welcome to him.' Meghan tossed out the challenge to gauge her response.

Claire came alive at her throwaway suggestion. 'You're letting on!'

Meghan shrugged. 'No. I'm perfectly serious.'

'Well, that's powerful news for sure.' Claire's lovely brown eyes sparkled.

Meghan hid a smile at her gullibility. Claire and Dermot? Who knew? She felt only the slightest twinge of betrayal between her two good friends. On reflection though, it was a relief and made perfect sense. Claire loved good times while someone else paid the bills. She frowned. But would Dermot consider Claire worthy enough? Her friend was certainly gorgeous. Stunning figure. Loved the social life. Glamming up.

A surge of protection rose up in her. If Dermot O'Brien mistreated or neglected her impressionable friend, she'd personally sort him out. Still, if that was the way the wind was blowing — and Claire certainly appeared interested, if not smitten — she hoped it worked out for them. It would make telling Dermot easier when she returned to Ireland, realising he had moved on. And with the news, she now felt no guilt in her own attraction toward Dusty. In a moment of revelation, Meghan realised that if Claire was interested in Dermot, she was less likely to blab that he was engaged.

If Dusty knew, she would lose him. He would believe she'd lied and belonged to another. Meghan couldn't bear the thought. She would hate leaving him most of all when she returned to Ireland. Would he care? There was definitely a *thing* going on between them and so far he hadn't shown interest in another woman. Local gossip would be rife about widower Nash if he did.

She'd never felt this sense of passion with Dermot. Was that how you knew it was real love? That if you lost the other person you wouldn't feel whole? That half of you would be missing? She only grasped the lack of feeling with Dermot since knowing Dusty. It was all about magnets and chemistry, and you couldn't do a thing about it. Not that she'd want to.

Focusing on Claire again, who had looked equally absorbed in thought as they sipped the last of their wine, Meghan saw her friend and each of their changing lives through fresh eyes.

'How long can you stay?' she asked. Knowing Claire, she suspected it might not be too long. She would grow bored out here, and restless. Besides, Dermot might be drawing her back sooner than even Claire knew herself.

'I hadn't really thought about it or

planned anything,' Claire admitted.

'You realise I'm working weekdays and will only be free to spend time with you after school and weekends.'

'I didn't think of that. Can't you get time off?'

Meghan shook her head. 'Spring holidays aren't for a few weeks yet. You're welcome to use my car if you want to drive back to the coast for a day or two. Or we could go together at the weekend?'

Meghan was hesitant to suggest it with so much happening soon. The Sunday Plains open day garden fundraiser for one thing. She still had lots more baking she wanted to do, but Claire wouldn't appreciate spending time with her in a kitchen.

Meghan prepared a light meal for them both. To her surprise, sociable Claire retired early. Meghan thanked the long international flight and took advantage of a few quiet hours. She closed the hallway door against noise and set to baking for a few hours to fend off her frustration and anxiety at so much confusion in her life right now.

Next day, after her usual early morning run while Claire slept, Meghan left a note and her car keys on the dining table and walked to school. The heavy pungent smell of wattle clung to the air, promising spring. She welcomed the warmer sunshine and had already forsaken winter clothes for light long skirts and tops, patting a large straw hat over her unruly auburn hair.

She returned home during her lunch break at midday to find Claire and the car gone but a note in her friend's beautiful scripted handwriting to meet her at the pub.

The familiar tanned and bearded face of Steve glanced up from behind the rustic bar and smiled as Meghan entered its cool thick-walled interior. 'What's with the Irish invasion?' he chuckled, nodding toward a window table.

Meghan's heart rolled over with pleasure and sank with dismay at the same time. Claire was sitting cosily close to a devastatingly handsome Dusty, smiling and blathering on to him as though they were old friends. What were the odds in this small town that those two people should meet again? Maybe simply because it *was* small.

Meghan briefly closed her eyes and took a deep breath. Whatever fate dealt, she would survive. Still, she felt sick in her stomach, hoping Claire hadn't blurted out anything about her engagement. As she strolled toward them, Dusty caught her arrival, their gazes met and he rose at her approach.

'Meghan,' he murmured. Her body responded with an ache of pleasure at the gesture and the sight of him.

'Meggie!' Claire squealed. 'It only took me fifteen minutes to drive around the *whole* town,' she gushed with her usual drama and humour, 'so I made myself comfortable in here. And who should wander in but this very handsome fella. Beer is a bit pale, though, compared to our black stuff.' She held up her glass and wrinkled her nose.

'But it slides down well enough in this heat.'

Meghan noticed Dusty's drink was empty, then grinned at Claire's comment. Today was only a warm spring day. She'd been warned by the locals that summer delivered much more punch and was slowly bracing herself for the months ahead.

Claire patted the chair beside her, opposite Dusty. 'Sit yourself down and join us.'

Meghan obliged, feeling like an intruder. 'Glad you've entertained yourself. Dusty.' She glanced up at him towering beside her. 'Still in town?'

'Heading back soon. Can I get you a drink?'

'Just a dry ginger ale, thanks. I have an afternoon's teaching ahead of me.'

When he returned with her frosted glass, he remained standing.

'Will you not join us for lunch?' Claire begged, flashing him a broad smile.

'I'm afraid I have a long drive and

work at the end of it.'

'That's no fun,' Claire teased, shaping her lips into a cheeky pout. 'You're sounding like our Dermot. All work and no play.'

Meghan was sure her heart stopped beating for a moment. 'A mutual friend,' she explained quickly at Dusty's raised eyebrows of query. 'Claire, we should order,' she went on. 'I have a class straight after lunch.'

Luckily, Claire was easily distracted and made no further comment.

'I'll leave you girls to catch up. Claire, nice to meet you again. Meghan, I'll see you out home for the garden party. Beth will catch you up on the details.'

When he smiled, her heart tumbled. 'Sure. I look forward to it.' *More than you know*, Meghan thought, watching him stride away. She reined in her feelings toward him to avoid questions from Claire, but a little of her heart went with him as he disappeared from view.

'A garden party.' Claire brightened. 'With dressing up and hats and all?'

Meghan burst out laughing. 'Outback style, yes. People come from hours around.'

Claire frowned over the odd expression. 'When is it?'

'Two weeks,' Meghan said as their fish, chips and salad arrived.

'Oh.' Claire's slender white shoulders sagged in disappointment. 'I might not be here that long.'

'That's a shame. You doing more travelling while you're in Australia, then?'

'Oh, no.' Claire's eyes widened, appalled by the thought. 'I'm going straight back home.'

'You came all this way just to see me? I'm staggered you could get time off work.'

Claire had the grace to shuffle in discomfort as she picked at her salad, suddenly appearing to have lost her appetite. 'Actually, I'm free at the moment. I gave up my job,' she said quietly.

Meghan's eyebrows rose high. 'You're

letting on! Why?'

'Dermot said my talents were wasted in a small shop. I'm applying for managerial positions in Dublin,' she revealed proudly.

Without any experience? Meghan almost blurted out. 'A dress shop in Rathdrum is a mite different to one in the city.'

'Dermot says I have the looks and the presentation,' she defended.

Meghan grew indignant for Claire. *And he's pushing and moulding you the same way he tried with me. He's grooming a new protégé. While we're still engaged.* Meghan wished Dermot was man enough to call off their engagement himself. Pride, she guessed. Meghan had walked away, so he was making her return and face him. Well, it would certainly be with his ring but without an apology.

Meghan reached out for Claire's hand across the pub table and gave it a squeeze. 'Do what's in your heart, Claire. Not what someone else tells you to do.'

To her frustration, Claire just stared

naively. Every woman's time with Dermot O'Brien ran a similar course. She pictured her friend's future and prayed she either met his challenge head-on or saw the light.

After lunch, as the women hovered under the pub veranda, Meghan said, 'I should be home by five.'

'What am I supposed to do all afternoon?' Claire whined.

Meghan shrugged. 'There's a heated pool in the sports complex. You can raid my cupboard and borrow my swimmers.'

Claire turned up her nose. 'I prefer looking at water rather than being in it.'

No point in heading for the coast at the weekend then. 'You could drive out any of the roads from town and check out the wildflowers. They're looking powerful grand at the moment.'

Hardly riveting amusements for a bubbly woman who preferred shopping and city lights.

'There's nothing else?' Claire asked hopefully.

Meghan shook her head. 'It's the outback, Claire. What did you expect?'

'Honestly, I had no idea. I didn't think you'd be so far away from everything.'

'Well, I hope you're not too bored. See you tonight.' She smiled and waved as she headed back to school.

It hardly surprised Meghan that within days, not weeks, Claire grew fidgety. There was far less to occupy her time in the outback than in Dublin, and Mallawa pub was her only social outlet. Filled with mostly men, it *did* have its attractions. Old or young, they were tanned and muscled, but they were hardly Claire's type.

Listening to her instincts, Meghan suggested she drive Claire to Geraldton to spend a few days on the coast and return for her the following weekend. But Claire just shrugged. 'Didn't look to be much there when I was flying in.'

Meghan tried again. 'How about Perth, then?'

Claire cheered up and too readily

agreed. 'That makes more sense.'

'Except you'd have to come all the way back up here again,' Meghan pointed out. She paused. 'To be honest, Claire, you don't think it's too grand out here, do you?'

Claire looked regretful. 'Sorry.'

'Do you have a return ticket to Ireland?'

Claire nodded. 'Open but undated.'

'If you're missing home, why don't you just book a flight then?' Meghan suggested carefully.

'You're not offended?'

'It's been wonderful seeing you, Claire. Honest. But the outback's not for everyone.' Her concentration drifted. 'When I got stuck out on the road with a flat tyre the first day I arrived, I was horrified. Then I forced myself to just stand still and take a good look at the place. It was amazing.'

Claire looked utterly sceptical.

So less than a week after Claire had arrived, the women were hunched over Meghan's laptop checking flights back to Dublin through Singapore and London. This time, Claire didn't seem ruffled by the stopovers and being stuck for another twenty hours on planes. Because they had booked a late Saturday afternoon flight, it meant an early start driving back to the coast for Claire to catch her domestic flight from Geraldton in time to meet her international connection through Perth.

So it was all a bit of a rush. The night before, they hardly slept, but for different reasons. Claire with the excitement of repacking, although she virtually flung everything wildly back into her suitcase. And Meghan eagerly anticipating the upcoming weekend open day out at Sunday Plains.

With Claire happy to be heading home, the conversation with Meghan in the car out to the coast was relaxed. They blathered on about anything, turned up the radio loud and wound down the windows to let the warm spring wind whip their hair about in the cross breeze.

At the airport, they laughed and cried at the same time.

'Promise me we'll get as full as a bingo bus on a Friday night when you come home for Christmas,' Claire pleaded.

Meghan watched her friend's jaunty swing as she walked across the tarmac to her commuter plane. It was a bittersweet moment because Claire's telling visit had shifted the dynamics in all their lives. Yet, as different as Meghan and Claire were, they would always be friends. Their very contrasting personalities and blunt honesty with each other meant any disagreements flared quickly but soon fizzled.

With Claire's departure Meghan sighed, turned her little car inland and headed back to Mallawa.

8

During the following week when Meghan had barely returned from her run one morning, protected these days by her straw hat and a long-sleeved shirt, Beth phoned. Not the most promising start to her day.

'About the open garden day,' Beth plunged straight into business without any pleasantries.

'My freezer and biscuit tins are all full,' Meghan said brightly.

Beth ignored her attempt at friendliness. 'I'm driving out to the homestead this weekend for a final check before our big days the weekend after. Dusty thinks you should come out, too. See how everything works.'

She sounded none too pleased or enthusiastic, but Meghan overlooked her indifference because Dusty had issued the invitation. 'That's fine. I'm free.' She matched Beth's coolness.

'Sally's coming into town to collect Ollie after school to take him back to Bindi, so there'll be just the two of us. Can you be ready by five?'

'Yes. I'll pack up all my food and bring it out.'

'Until Friday then.' She hung up.

Meghan sighed. The trip out to Sunday Plains trapped in a vehicle with Beth for an hour promised to be demanding. But the prospect of seeing Dusty again lifted her heart, although he still clung to the past and didn't appear in any hurry to move on.

So, on her morning run the next day, her pace slowed as she approached the cemetery. She glanced around to see if anyone was about this early, watching, and felt foolish. She didn't normally talk to dead people. Today, she felt the need. Meghan found the grave and knelt down on the hard stony ground. She took a deep breath and began.

'Hi, Alison. You don't know me, but my name's Meghan Dorney and I think

I'm falling in love with your husband. I hail all the way from Ireland. I came out here teaching, expecting to stay for six months and then go home.'

She smiled and cast her gaze around the deserted cemetery, then glanced up at the clear blue outback sky. 'If your spirit is out there somewhere and if you're listening, please let Dusty go. Please. Send him a sign,' she pleaded urgently. 'Send him to me.'

Before she left, Meghan closed her eyes. She wasn't a particularly religious person but believed there was *something* out there. So she offered up a silent prayer to whoever might be listening. Just in case. You never knew.

* * *

On Friday when Beth arrived, they interacted like strangers, making only necessary and idle small talk as Meghan loaded her food containers and overnight bag into the back of the four-wheel drive for the journey out to Sunday Plains.

Beth was behind the wheel and had the engine running before Meghan barely had a chance to click on her seatbelt. She found the older woman's frosty attitude distressing. Only the thought of Dusty at the other end made it bearable. She didn't expect any conversation so they drove in silence for miles until the magic of spring in the outback lowered Beth's guard and left Meghan speechless. The further they travelled, the more breathtaking the landscape.

Such a huge change had taken place since she was last out here. Then, it had been clothed in winter green and she had really only glimpsed it in the dusk. This wonderland of pink everlastings made her feel like an excited child. Such a prolific mantle spread over the countryside.

Meghan had brought her camera and longed to ask Beth to stop so she could take some photos, but was reluctant to ask even though she sensed a mellowing of the other woman's mood since leaving town.

'Oh,' Meghan gasped at the endless carpet of wildflowers as far as you could see. 'This is amazing.'

'Yes, it's something else,' Beth breathed almost reverently, constantly glancing out the window as she drove. The sealed bitumen road before them was like a grey ribbon through an infinite mass of colour. 'Even after living out here for a lifetime it's still a delight,' Beth admitted quietly.

Meghan knew a moment of mutual appreciation with her at the sight of the natural splendour stretching out around them. For a while, the tension eased. Even at this late hour of the day, they weren't alone on the roads. They encountered tourists in caravans, four-wheel drives and motor homes all travelling the outback for a glimpse of the magical wildflower season.

Finally Beth slowed and turned off onto the rough gravelled track leading to Sunday Plains. When they rattled over the ramp Meghan checked her enthusiasm, remembering it was only about ten minutes from here to the homestead. She saw the windmill first, then the grain silos and machinery sheds, until the green oasis surrounding the homestead emerged.

Beth swung around the circular drive and pulled up in front. It was hard not to notice the arresting man long before they stopped. He was waiting and easily took two steps at a time down from the veranda to meet them.

'Hi,' he drawled as Meghan stepped out and stretched. 'Welcome back.'

In a black T-shirt and hip-hugging jeans, he was one dreamboat of a man. His gaze slid appreciatively over her floaty floral maxi-dress and loafers but he made no move to touch. She lived in hope her prayer would be answered.

'Grand to be here again. Country's nothing short of fabulous at the moment.'

He smiled in understanding, then strode around the front of the vehicle. 'Mother.' He greeted her with a quick hug and kiss on the cheek.

'Heaps of boxes to unload.' Beth popped the rear door with the remote.

As Dusty grabbed a handful, Meghan swung a quick glance around the garden. Beth and the workmen had excelled. Sunset stretched shining fingers of citrus light between the grand shady old trees and across the lawns. The smell of freshly mown grass lingered on the twilight air. Drifts of lavender hedges sent out their musky scent and a rich costume of spring flowers cloaked the garden. Meghan was lost in its tranquillity and beauty.

'Come on in,' Dusty said halfway up the steps.

The women gathered up more boxes and headed for the house. The two border collies panted excitedly on the veranda.

'Hey, fellas.' Meghan shuffled her containers to one arm and bent to fondle their silky heads and ears. 'How have you been?' Two pairs of dark brown eyes regarded her with adoration.

The screen door whined and slammed behind her. Inside the long cool hallway, Meghan followed Dusty and Beth down to the kitchen and her appetite kicked in at the heavenly smell of cooking meat.

'Barbeque's on already,' Dusty said. 'Steak, sausages, and plenty of onion. Did you remember the salad?' he asked his mother.

'Of course.'

Dusty frowned at her sharp reply. 'Just asking. You seem . . . tired.'

'It's been a busy week,' she snapped.

'Then I order an early night,' he countered.

'Maybe.'

From the landscape windows overlooking the rear courtyard and garden to the horizon far beyond, Meghan drank in the enviable view. She was so aware of Dusty in the room and the sound of his deep voice behind her, she was almost afraid to face him. He would see the longing in her eyes. When she swung about, she saw only gentlemanly regard in his gaze and nothing more. She told herself she was content with that, but a cheeky little voice in her head whispered, *Liar*.

Meghan settled into the background when they ate dinner outdoors on the patio. Any other time or alone with Dusty, she might have savoured it more, but she found the dynamics of their small trio stifling with Beth continually irritable and any attempts she made at polite conversation clipped with some retort. Meghan wasn't the only one affected. Dusty also regarded his mother with frowning concern.

He had poured them all a lovely chilled rosé so she concentrated on enjoying her tender steak, draining her glass of wine and readily accepting another when Dusty offered.

Later, to their amazed relief and Dusty's insistence, Beth retired early.

'Meghan and I can clear up.'

She grumbled but obeyed. 'I'll be up at first light tomorrow. There's a lot to get done,' she flung ungraciously over her shoulder as she left.

They worked together in comfortable silence to stack the dishwasher and tidy the kitchen until Dusty boiled the kettle and cut some slabs of fruitcake onto a plate. 'Let's take these out onto the front veranda.'

They settled opposite each other in comfortable wicker chairs with padded cushions. The solar garden lights cast their soft glow into corners and lit up the peeling bark on gum-tree trunks.

'Did your friend Claire enjoy her visit?'

Meghan finished her mouthful of cake and flashed him a grin. 'She barely lasted a week. But it was wonderful to see someone from home.'

'You're not homesick?' he asked softly.

'Good heavens, no. The past few months have been the most amazing time in my life.' The warm night breeze rose, rippled the hem of her long skirt and played with strands of her hair. 'You're so lucky to be living out here.

There's a rugged peace in the outback.'

'Not everyone feels it.' Dusty set down his empty mug and leaned forward, clasping his hands together. 'I'm worried about Mum,' he said quietly.

'She has seemed strained lately,' Meghan agreed.

'She refuses help and is determined to keep the garden open day going because it's such a huge fundraiser for the community.'

'Gardening is her passion and she loves doing it. It must also give her satisfaction and purpose.'

He frowned and paused. 'I wonder if I might ask a favour of you.'

Anything on this earth. 'Of course.'

'She'll never admit it, but I think it's time for Mum to share the load. She's been the driving force for the garden party every year, but she's finding it more difficult to manage alone. If she agrees — ' He pulled a wry grin. ' — and I'm not looking forward to that conversation, would you be prepared to step in? Could you handle taking orders from her? Be her right-hand woman next weekend?'

'Willingly, but she'll never agree.' Meghan shook her head. 'She's too independent.'

He shrugged. 'I'll take her aside and at least suggest it.'

'Good luck with that.' She chuckled.

'Could you handle an early-morning ride tomorrow?'

'Absolutely.'

'Daybreak?'

'Grand. Best time to be out, I've found, for my morning run before the day gets too warm.'

He seemed amused by her enthusiasm. 'Bring your camera.' He pushed himself to his feet and held out a hand toward her. She grasped it and he pulled her up, tugging her closer, still holding her hand. He seemed unsure what to do next but eventually brushed a lingering kiss on her cheek and murmured, 'Thanks for offering to help Mum.'

'If she'll accept it.'

'I've taken your bag into one of the guest rooms. I'll show you the way.' At her door, he stepped aside and leant against the doorframe. 'Bathroom's next door.'

'Thanks.' She paused. 'Good night.'

Her hesitation was worth it. This time he knew exactly what he was doing. He leaned in until the outline of his face loomed over her and kissed her warm and full on the mouth.

'Sweet dreams,' he drawled.

'I'm sure they will be.'

★　★　★

It was still dark next morning and Meghan was just stirring when she heard the promised soft knock on her door from Dusty. She scrambled from bed, pulled on comfortable riding slacks and a long-sleeved shirt, and grabbed her straw hat hanging on the back of her bedroom door.

Dusty waited in the kitchen, backed

up against a counter, arms crossed. 'Morning.'

'I feel like one of my students playing truant,' she chuckled.

'Horses are saddled but you won't be needing that.' He nodded toward her hat. 'I have a surprise for you out in the stables.'

'Have you now?'

Intrigued, she followed. Sensing action, Queenie and Butch weren't far behind. In the first hint of dawn that washed the sky with pale light, Meghan saw their mounts tethered to a fence. Dusty reached over to a post and retrieved a broad-brimmed sandy-coloured hat with a black plaited band similar to the favourite battered one she often saw him wearing outdoors.

'Your own Akubra. Should tame that hair of yours and keep the sun off your freckles.' He settled it onto her head, stood back and grinned.

'Thank you,' she acknowledged the thoughtful gift warmly. 'I love it. I feel like a regular Aussie now.'

'You're welcome,' he said softly, handing her the reins of the nearest horse.

'Does this ride have a purpose then?'

'Apart from grabbing you for an hour before Mum corners you all day, there's something I want to show you.'

It was nothing short of wonderful to be astride again. They headed out one of the red dirt tracks away from the homestead. The crisp air gave no hint of the heat to come later in the day. They cantered for a while across lush paddocks where sheep grazed in the distance and looked up idly as they passed. The dogs stayed with them until they reached a sparsely wooded area on a gentle rise. The sun had just breached the horizon and morning light gleamed over everything.

Meghan gasped, pulled up and jumped from her horse, leaving the reins dangling. 'Awesome.' She beamed. Impatiently, she snatched her camera from the saddle-bag and wandered off, knee-deep in wildflowers.

Dusty contemplated her with a soft

indulgent smile, dismounted and backed up against a gum tree. She was aware of being watched but forced her concentration on taking photographs. With both dogs racing and leaping around her, she tramped to the top of the hill, took off her hat to let the light breeze cool her damp hair, and turned a full circle.

After a moment Dusty joined her, squinting from beneath his hat out at the view. Sunday Plains homestead below basked in the sunshine, surrounded by its oasis of greenery.

'The countryside's so flat. Who knew you had hills?' she laughed.

When she glanced back at him, she caught her breath in alarm. Dusty's suntanned face was serious and his brown eyes held such tenderness it was frightening. She didn't move; barely breathed. *This* was what she had waited for. A sign of his affection and the courage to show it.

'I've missed you,' he said, sliding an arm about her waist and brushing red wisps away from her forehead to plant a kiss in their place.

They laughed at both dogs on their haunches, heads tilted, watching them with interest, which broke the tension.

He stalled. 'Meghan, it's probably bad timing . . . You're only here for a few more months . . . but I'd like to spend more time with you.'

The warmth in his plea was unnecessary. 'I'm up for it. You don't kiss a woman like you did after that weekend out at Bindi,' Meghan teased, 'then leave her guessing. Or is that how you outback men operate, then?'

'I'm out of practice.'

'Fair enough,' she whispered.

And then it was so simple to slide her arms up around his neck and allow herself to be thoroughly kissed.

'One day at a time?' he murmured.

She nodded. An understanding was all she sought for now, although she knew exactly what she felt in her heart.

Back at the homestead Beth was waiting, scowling over her coffee mug at the kitchen table as the pair stumbled laughing into the room.

'Took Meghan up to Benjamin's Rise,' Dusty explained easily.

'It's not always this idyllic.' Beth glared at Meghan in resentment. 'Summer is fierce.'

Meghan determined not to be discouraged. 'Knee-deep in snow back home isn't a whole keg of fun either.' She swapped a knowing grin with Dusty.

'So what's on your agenda this morning?' He glanced across at his mother.

'Show Meghan where everything is and how it should be organised for next weekend. We'll need to come out Thursday night to give us Friday to prepare and arrange everything beforehand. The district ladies will take charge of the kitchen, as usual. Sally will be here, of course.'

'Grand.' Meghan eagerly looked forward to catching up with her friend in person. Regular chinwags over the phone weren't quite the same.

★ ★ ★

After breakfast, Dusty took the dogs and disappeared in the utility, promising to be back for lunch. Meghan trailed Beth to a large brick store shed off the patio. She thought the padlock was overkill until Beth dragged the heavy wooden door open to reveal a huge cache of supplies.

'This is where we keep everything for the garden weekend from year to year. Dusty and his men will unload the heaviest boxes but we can start sorting through and taking some of it into the house.'

There were boxes of crockery, cutlery, white tablecloths, stacks of chairs, folded trestle tables and urns. Meghan's jaw dropped in amazement. 'How many people are you expecting?'

'Hundreds. Folk come from everywhere in the district. Some drive for hours just for the day. Even station owners whose children are sent away to school or are part of School of the Air still come to socialise and support us. At twenty dollars a head, that's potentially thousands of dollars available for the community.'

Meghan had learned soon after her arrival in the outback never to be amazed by the generosity and spirit of its people.

'So,' Meghan said, hands on hips, 'what's first, then?'

In relay they carted in lighter boxes and unpacked beautiful tea sets and cutlery, all of which had to be washed, so Meghan spent a while standing at the sink. When Dusty returned for lunch they took a thick salad sandwich and cuppa, sank into veranda chairs overlooking the front garden and discussed how best to lay out the tables and chairs; where shade fell all day; where table umbrellas might be needed.

The afternoon passed equally quickly opening and sorting more boxes. Dinner of leftover cold meats and salads was washed down with icy beer. Fresh fruit and yoghurt cream was served for afters. With Beth's mood at least civil, the evening was not entirely unpleasant. Then Dusty excused himself to make phone calls, leaving the women alone together.

Meghan made an effort at conversation. 'The garden is a picture, Beth. You've done a power of work.'

'People expect it,' she sighed. 'There's months of preparation.'

Beth's admission and weariness surprised her. Meghan wondered if she was just fulfilling tradition and expectations. 'If you're feeling overwhelmed, I'm happy to share the load.'

'I've been doing this for twenty years. I can manage perfectly well,' Beth bristled.

Meghan took a deep breath. 'I've worked in my parents pub for fourteen years. Sometimes you just feel swamped, but I've learned to ask for help. There's no shame in that.'

'I'll be fine,' she said stiffly.

'Dusty's worried about you.'

'So now he's confiding in you, is he?' Beth lurched to her feet and hurried indoors.

Meghan wished she hadn't said anything. Left alone to brood, she waited for Dusty's return. Eventually, he reappeared and sat beside her on the long timber seat, stretching out an arm behind.

'Mum looked troubled.'

'It was something I said,' Meghan groaned.

'Don't blame yourself.' He sought her hand and linked fingers. 'This happens every year. She drives herself until there's nothing left. Come on, let's take a walk.'

'In the dark?'

'I know where I'm going.'

And they did, arm in arm, but they ended up lingering and kissing more than walking and talking. Meghan marvelled how such a rugged man could be so tender. With such feelings buried deep, no wonder he had taken his wife's death so hard and had taken so long to recover.

★ ★ ★

Typically, just when Meghan was revelling in a weekend on Sunday Plains, it disappeared all too swiftly. Next day, a load of linen tablecloths had to be ironed and spread out carefully on a guest bed so they didn't crease.

Beth seemed less troubled today and wondered if Dusty had spoken to her, but an underlying distance remained between them. By late afternoon, Beth wanted to head back to town. Meghan reluctantly packed her bag and joined Dusty and his mother out on the front steps. He took her sadness and breath away when he kissed her in full view of his mother as though making his intentions clear.

'I'll come into town during the week. Maybe we could grab a meal at the pub.'

It sounded awfully like a date. Half her time here was over and she felt confused about leaving. 'Sure. Any time.'

At the car, Dusty said to his mother, 'I think Meghan should drive back to town. It's good experience for her, driving on outback roads.'

When Beth was about to protest, he dangled the keys he'd pilfered and handed them to Meghan. 'No arguments,' he said kindly. 'Just this once.'

'All right,' she muttered. 'Think you can find your way back to Mallawa?' she tossed at Meghan.

'GPS on my mobile phone,' she said with a grin.

Beth flashed her a glance of resignation, hugged Dusty and climbed into the passenger seat. Meghan climbed in behind the wheel feeling guilty for being the cause of another thorn in Beth's side. She hadn't known the woman in her youth but saw the struggle to keep pushing and doing what she'd always done. In Beth's eyes, concession would mean defeat.

They didn't speak for the entire return journey so Meghan merely said a polite good night, adding, 'See you out at the homestead on Friday.'

Beth's response was clipped. 'Early as you can. Best take our own cars.'

'Sure. See you then.'

Meghan made a note to have Gazza at the garage check over her vehicle before travelling out alone later in the week.

9

Next day before school, Meghan heard a knock on her back door. That ruled out Noreen and Cassie, who always breezed into her kitchen like family.

'Beth.' Meghan smiled but her heart sank. 'Come in.' She gestured warmly and stepped aside.

The older woman was smart in slacks and a blue checked shirt. Meghan still wore leggings and a long over-shirt from her morning run, her cloud of hair falling free around her shoulders. She felt daunted in the presence of this trim, confident woman.

'I know you need to get to school.' Beth glanced away. 'But I didn't sleep well last night and I need to say my piece.'

'Sure. I'll put the kettle on.'

'Don't bother.'

Meghan was jolted by her abrupt

tone. 'It's no bother.'

Beth primly took a seat. 'I didn't come for a pleasant chat and cup of tea.'

Meghan faced her across the table and waves of friction flowed across the brittle space between them.

Beth hesitated. 'Dusty clearly enjoys your company.'

So, straight into it then. Treading carefully, Meghan replied, 'I understand he's had a rough couple of years.'

'I don't want to see him suffer like that again.'

'I'm sure no one does.'

'I won't stand by and see him hurt. You're leaving.'

Meghan saw where this was heading. 'Not until the end of the year. A lot can happen in three months.'

'Dusty's still recovering from Alison's loss.'

'Are you sure?' Meghan challenged and Beth gasped.

'How dare you speak to me like that!'

'I dare because I had hoped we could be friends, and friends should be honest with each other. I'm not leading Dusty on. Our feelings are mutual. Ask him yourself.'

Beth glared, speechless. Meghan took advantage of her stunned silence to continue, 'He's finally taking steps toward his future. You should be applauding his courage, not holding him back. I'm surprised, having lost a spouse yourself, that your own experience hasn't allowed you to accept that life goes on for those left behind.'

Beth stared in surprise at Meghan's bold words, her mission thwarted, and her stony facade faltered.

More gently, Meghan went on, 'Dusty and I are really good friends for now, Beth. Enjoying each other's company. Knowing his history, I've let any approach come from him. I'm not in the habit of chasing and using men.' A quick image of Claire flashed across her mind. 'I respect your whole family, Beth. Sally and I have become close pals, too.'

Faced with Meghan's frankness,

Beth's hostility flickered. 'If you hurt him — '

'That would never be my intention.' Drawing on her own mother's wisdom, Meghan said, 'Aileen once told me that a parent's love can't solve a child's problems.' She paused. 'You can only be there for them. Something I'll try to remember when I have a family of my own.' She progressed to the issue on her mind. 'Are you concerned for yourself, perhaps, and not Dusty at all?'

Beth grew indignant. 'I can't think what you mean.'

'Beth,' she urged softly.

She had entered Meghan's kitchen ready for battle. Now she slumped back in her chair, her chilly demeanour gone. A long sigh escaped, leaving her looking unguarded and almost relieved. 'I've never talked to anyone about this,' she admitted. 'Everyone relies on me. I'm supposed to be strong.'

Aware this was a huge confession from Dusty's mother, Meghan jumped up to boil the kettle for a cuppa and opened a jar of crunchy oat biscuits, giving Beth time to gather her composure. The kettle soon whistled and Meghan made them strong coffee. With her back turned, she sent off an SMS to Barbara apologising that she would be late this morning.

'You don't have time for this.' Beth frowned anxiously, glancing at the wall clock nearing nine.

'I've notified Barbara. She'll understand.' She set their mugs and biscuits on the table. 'Something's on your mind. Let's get you sorted out, then.'

Beth stirred sugar and milk into her drink. 'Sally only ever wanted to marry Phil,' she began, 'so she was gone by the time she was twenty-one. And Sophie disappeared, wandering the world. But Dusty and I have always seemed to end up supporting each other. Just . . . circumstances. Especially after Dan died and Dusty was so young when he took over Sunday Plains.

'It was inevitable Dusty would marry, but it was still a wrench to move into

Mallawa and leave it all behind. Even after he married Alison, she was a career woman and often away, so I took up the slack. Did endless baking for him and manned the homestead during shearing and harvesting. It helped me as much as him to stay connected to the house that Dan and I built together and where we raised our family.' She shrugged. 'After Alison died, he needed me again. We needed each other. I just haven't wanted to break away,' she said in a small voice. 'I do still love that place so much. So many memories. So much life lived out there. The years just slid by,' she murmured.

Meghan smiled warmly and squeezed her hand. 'Go on.'

'I'm not a complete fool.' She smiled wanly, broke a biscuit and to Meghan's amusement, dunked it in her tea. 'I can see Dusty's ready to move on again, now. You've brought a positive change into his life, Meghan, but . . . ' Her voice wavered. ' . . . I'm afraid I'll be unwanted.'

Stunned by such a confession from an outwardly strong woman, Meghan understood now that Beth still bore the scars of her husband's loss from a decade before. She welcomed her grandson to stay in town all week as company for herself as much as for Ollie to socialise with his mates.

'You'll never lose Dusty or any of your children, Beth. You're a close family and your strong bonds can never be broken. Your son and daughters want and need you in their lives, that goes without saying. It's more about sharing their lives now maybe, and not being responsible for them, whatever form that takes. Don't you sometimes want time to yourself?' she suggested gently.

'I'd rather be frantic than idle.'

Beth was terrified of being alone! 'Fair play to you but, actually, I think you just try to do too much.' Like Dusty, Meghan had noticed a weariness about Beth sometimes. She still pushed herself when perhaps it wasn't always necessary. But she understood it gave her a sense of purpose. Meghan thought of Dusty losing his wife and Sally's own difficulties in having the large family she craved. Beth was there for them through all of it and shared the emotional load.

Beth managed a weak smile of resignation. 'You're probably right, and you've read me well. I keep busy so I don't have time to stop and think,' she admitted. 'Thank you for being honest and listening. I've never wanted to make a fuss or grumble. The children's troubles always seemed more important.'

After their frank discussion, Meghan felt a huge burden lifted in their friendship and shrugged. 'Sometimes it's easier to have a chinwag with a stranger.'

'You're hardly that, my dear. And I'll work on trying to feel easier in my own company.'

★　★　★

Dusty phoned the following night, and Wednesday twilight saw them holding hands and strolling down to the pub for a drink. After a deliciously personal welcome kiss first, of course, at her house when he arrived.

Dusty ordered a beer and Meghan a crisp chardonnay that apparently came from down south in the Margaret River wine region. Their entrance drew an interested glance from publican Steve, and nods and smiles from other local patrons.

Dusty proved uncomfortable. They had barely chatted for thirty minutes when he said, 'Do you mind if we don't stay for dinner? I could do without an audience.'

This great big man was shy of gossip? Meghan grinned to herself in amusement. 'Not at all.'

'Walk you home?'

'I can't promise there's much food in the house at the moment. I've no idea what we're going to eat.'

'Surprise me,' he chuckled.

No, you've surprised me, Meghan thought.

'I don't expect a feast, Meghan,' he drawled, following her into the kitchen.

'You won't be getting it tonight. It's just leftovers,' she laughed.

It seemed crazy to have nerves when she'd never felt more comfortable with a man in her life and she'd wanted to see him again so badly. She clamped down on her rising hopes and excitement about this man. It was September and, as she'd told Beth on Monday morning, anything could happen before the end of the year. She didn't want to jinx this wonderful new blossoming friendship before it had barely started.

She decided to respect the privacy of Beth's confidences, so she didn't say anything. In time, Beth would feel more willing to ask for help and learn to delegate.

Meghan regarded the strong, quiet man sharing her kitchen. 'How about vegetable patties with salad?'

'Perfect.'

'Wine or beer?'

'Can I get it?'

Meghan nodded toward the refrigerator. 'Beer's on the bottom shelf and I'll have a glass of the wine.'

She shredded the vegetables, lightly steamed and mashed them then added flour, herbs and eggs to form patties. While they gently fried, Dusty sipped his beer and watched her. Meghan felt herself blush. To avoid his gaze she moved past him and set two places at the table. When she turned he had risen and blocked her path.

'Dinner in five,' she breathed.

'Too busy for a kiss?'

She swallowed. 'Never.'

It broke the built up tension between them and satisfied a shared need to realise it was what they both craved of each other, but hesitated to be the first one to show it.

'I want to know everything about you,' he murmured against her hair while she was still in his arms.

'Not much to tell, so it won't take

211

long,' she quipped, then sent him an apologetic smile. 'Patties need turning.'

He sighed and she reluctantly slipped from his slackened embrace.

The evening became one of laughter, good-natured conversation and banter. Once they had cleared the air with that rewarding kiss, Meghan only marvelled at how naturally and easily they harmonised with each other. She told him all about her family, life and friends in Rathdrum, carefully omitting any mention of Dermot just yet. He asked her about teaching and Dorney's pub.

'Your turn,' she said eventually as they were cuddled together on the sofa later, mellowed and comfortable together in this new awakening in their relationship.

She didn't expect him to talk about Alison. That would happen in his own time. But he charmed her with tales of boyhood growing up on an outback station with two pesky sisters who, from the warm tone of his voice, he plainly adored. His sense of freedom, learning how to handle guns, losing his father too soon. The difficult years while still young and inexperienced, learning to run Sunday Plains and watching his mother grieve.

Meghan noticed he went no further in his life but stopped there. Shutting down any further confidences.

'I have a proposition for you,' Dusty said as he prepared to leave.

'I'm listening.'

'How would you feel about some *real* camping? I mean middle of nowhere, few comforts and under canvas?'

If it meant being with Dusty, she'd pretty much have a go at anything. 'Sounds like fun.'

'I'd like to take you out to the hills.' Meghan raised her eyebrows in disbelief and he chuckled. 'Yes, Benjamin Rise isn't the only one out here. They're actually ironstone rock formations in a national park. And the best and highest views are from the outcrops.' He paused. 'Interested?'

'Absolutely. Sounds grand.'

He reached out for her hand and

squeezed it. 'No strings. We'll each have our own tent and I'll bring all the gear.'

He didn't need to reassure her but she appreciated the gesture. She trusted this rugged man unconditionally with her life. 'I look forward to it.'

His steady gaze settled over her. 'You should see as much of the countryside as possible while you're here.'

She took his point but didn't enjoy being reminded of her limited time in the outback. The weeks were turning into months and slipping by fast enough. Thinking positively, Meghan realised Dusty was right though. She should make the most of it but she knew in her heart, when the time came, it was going to be a hard wrench leaving this distinctive part of the world and its people. One in particular.

'When would we go?'

'Weekend after the garden party?'

They kissed again, a warm and lingering taste of each other. One of Dusty's hands drifted into her loose tangle of hair and he just quietly held her during which they both basked in the moment. Meghan closed her eyes, nuzzled into his neck and kissed him there. Growing familiar with the scent of him until, with a small moan of resignation, he pulled away.

On her back doorstep in the dark, still tingling all over with warmth from yet another blistering good-night kiss, Meghan frowned. 'Mallawa's an awfully big town, so it is.' She poured on her Irish accent. 'Careful you don't get lost now on your way back to Beth's.'

'I have GPS on my mobile,' he said equally seriously.

They both burst out laughing.

'I'd offer to drive you but after half a bottle of wine, it would be just my Irish luck to meet the only policeman in town and be asked for a breath test.'

'The walk will do me good,' he said gallantly.

As he strolled away, his big athletic body gradually swallowed up by the dark, Meghan tried not to worry over the future and what it might hold.

Instead she focused on the promised camping trip ahead.

★ ★ ★

After her warm and blissful date with Dusty, it was less than forty-eight hours later when Meghan packed yet another overnight bag and headed for Sunday Plains at daybreak Friday morning. She'd sent Dusty a text to let him know when she left and secretly hoped to beat Beth.

The landscape was its usual amazing sea of colour and she had to slow down more than once when a kangaroo hopped across the road in front of her. Sunrise and sunset were their feeding times so she took care as she drove.

As she finally approached the homestead, Meghan noticed an enormous white marquee erected on the edge of the front lawns to one side. And Beth's four-wheel drive was already parked on the gravel! Meghan shook her head. The older woman might be forced to slow down, but she wouldn't do it without a fight. Dusty ambled from the house, grinning, so she leapt from her vehicle into his arms.

'All ready for work, I see.' His admiring gaze flowed over the denim shorts, white tank top and sneakers.

His athletic body was just as appealing in cargos, a T-shirt and bush sandals. With their arms around each other, they walked toward the house, patting the dogs as they excitedly danced around her ankles.

'Why the big tent?' she glanced back over her shoulder.

Dusty paused on the first step. 'After I left you on Wednesday night, Beth announced that the information office in town was promoting the garden open weekend and coach-loads of tourists are coming out. So I hired the marquee just in case.'

'Sounds like we're going to need it.'

'Looks like being a special year all round.' Dusty's eyes glinted with mischief.

Meghan felt herself blush and deflected his charm. 'Beth's here already. She must have left in the dark!'

'She was here with the sunrise. She's whipping up scrambled eggs and French toast.'

Meghan chuckled but her stomach rumbled at the thought. She'd only grabbed a coffee before she left. 'I'll go in and help her.'

In the kitchen, when Beth turned at Meghan's arrival and beamed, Dusty's eyebrows rose in query. When they hugged and greeted each other warmly, Meghan flashed him a devilish wink.

'Sally just phoned. Her tribe's on their way,' Beth announced as the women worked in harmony amassing piles of eggs and bacon and sprinkling the fried toast in cinnamon sugar.

Within fifteen minutes Sally, Phil and Ollie erupted into the kitchen for the family's first reunion since the Bindi weekend. Dusty ruffled his nephew's blond curls and Ollie just grinned. The men shook hands and the women hugged. After a long, noisy breakfast during which everyone caught up on news, Dusty pulled Meghan aside.

'How did you manage it?'

'What?' she teased.

'Mum.'

'A little Aussie charm I learned from you, and some Irish blarney.'

And then it was all hands to helping. Tables were set up on the lawns and in the tent, the crisp white cloths laid over them with protective plastic covers to be removed in the morning, and umbrellas erected. Dusty frequently went missing, checking the weekend forecast on the radio and computer.

A bank of urns and trays of cutlery were filled, and pretty floral serviettes and paper plates laid out. Ollie and Phil draped streamers and pumped balloons, tying them in bunches among the trees and inside the tent.

'It's all coming alive,' Meghan said eagerly at lunch when they all collapsed to take a break. 'It's going to be grand.'

'And busy,' Beth murmured beside

her. 'The kitchen ladies will arrive this evening and camp out ready for an early start tomorrow.'

In the afternoon, the women sliced and mixed fillings for sandwiches, sausage rolls and all manner of tasty hot savouries. The cakes, slices and biscuits were thawed and cut up but left in their containers ready for the local helpers to assemble plates in the morning.

'How early do visitors start coming?' Meghan asked.

'Be spruced up early,' Sally warned with a chuckle. 'Some locals arrive after breakfast and make a day of it.'

Toward evening, Dusty and Phil took charge of the barbeque. Through her guest-room window as she freshened and changed from her grubby working clothes to a long sundress, the first clouds of dust signalled the arrival of tomorrow's helpers. Dusty and his workmen erected roped-off areas in the homestead paddocks to control parking and camping.

After dinner, Dusty stole Meghan

away for a walk and they headed down to the helper camp where everyone gathered around a campfire drinking and talking, with someone strumming a guitar, others humming or tapping their feet to the music. Meghan was introduced and welcomed, and sat beside Dusty on a log. Noticing her stifled yawn, they said their farewells. Hand in hand, they ambled back to the homestead, its warm lights spilling from windows in welcome.

Everyone retired early, and Meghan felt like she had just fallen asleep when she heard movement in her room and the curtains were flung back.

'Rise and shine, Sleeping Beauty,' Dusty chuckled as he left.

'You're cruel,' she muttered, rolling over. Then Ollie ran in and jumped on her and she had no choice. Meghan bolted upright and, pretending to be fierce, said, 'Oliver Barnes, if your mother put you up to this, she's for it!' She leapt from bed and chased him as he squealed with delight.

She ignored the amused faces in the kitchen. 'I can have breakfast in my pyjamas,' she said, then noticed three strange ladies in the room. She pulled up and gulped back a mild dose of embarrassment. 'Good morning.'

'Meghan Dorney, this is Elaine, Julie and Marg,' Dusty said. He nodded toward the window, smirking. 'And the first visitors are here.'

'You're letting on!' Meghan gasped and fled for her bedroom but not before she heard one of the women say, 'That hair's as red as the dirt out in your paddocks, Dusty.'

Filled with devilment, Meghan stuck her head back around the door and said, 'Well, I should blend right in then, shouldn't I?'

She left them all shaking with gales of laughter.

Then the day, already in first gear, quickly revved into overdrive. Vehicles of all descriptions coated with red dust began appearing along the homestead track. Women in lovely summery dresses and light hats emerged, often escorted by men in traditional country gear of moleskins and checked shirts.

Meghan estimated that over the course of the weekend she must have walked heaps of kilometres out and back to the kitchen delivering endless cups of tea and coffee, and plates of scrumptious food.

The tourist coaches lumbered in just before midday and the occupants filled the tents. Every seat at every table under the trees, all over the lawns and beneath the verandas, was occupied. When people weren't strolling and admiring Beth's immaculate spring garden, they were eating, drinking or standing about chatting socially. Cameras clicked everywhere. Beth answered endless botanical questions and played hostess, renewing friendships with neighbours she might not have seen for a year.

The family and helpers were exhausted by late Sunday when camping tents were dismantled and the last cars trailed off down the track. Dwindling excitement settled over the homestead and weary satisfaction glowed on every face.

'That's the biggest crowd ever,' Beth announced, head back, eyes closed, resting in a recliner chair.

'Sure felt like it,' Sally agreed, as Phil rubbed her feet while she sprawled out on sofa in the lounge where everyone had subsided to recover.

Dusty had drawn Meghan down beside him and wrapped an arm around her shoulder where her head rested. Both legs ached and she'd never felt more tired or happy in her life.

'That was harder than a day in Dorney's pub,' Meghan said. 'You must have made a grand profit, Beth.'

She beamed. 'I couldn't have done it without all of you and the volunteers.'

They shared a knowing glance, Meghan sensing this was the beginning of Beth Nash loosening the reins and easing into the background. Somehow they all reluctantly found the energy to pack up, sort themselves out and prepare to leave.

'Beth's staying on here for a few days,' Dusty said as they strolled arm in arm in the dusk toward her parked car.

It wasn't until they had surfaced from an amorous goodbye kiss that Meghan glanced over Dusty's shoulder and realised they had a grinning audience on the veranda. Sally laughed and gave her the thumbs up. Meghan's cheeks still burned with embarrassment as she drove away.

10

A few days later, Meghan caught sight of Sally already seated in the Boomerang Cafe where they had arranged to meet, fondly known by locals as the Boomer. The small rustic cafe with its paved courtyard under shade sails and polished timber tables and chairs also boasted a gift shop of local crafts, gifts and souvenirs. Meghan proudly noticed Carrie's photography postcards on display.

She edged her way over and hugged her friend but, with only an hour from school for lunch, they placed their orders.

'Crumbed fish and salad for me,' Meghan told the waitress.

'And I'll have a toasted club sandwich.' Sally waved an arm. 'The whole district buzzes in wildflower season. Then before we know it, there's harvest and Christmas.'

Meghan's thought were on the end of semester, the imminent closing school year, and leaving. It didn't bear consideration at all. The food and a pot of tea arrived so they tucked in.

After a while Sally could no longer contain her curiosity. 'Well, give.'

'What about?' Meghan pretended ignorance, keeping Sally waiting.

Sally gasped in exasperation. 'You know what! My big brother. Things are looking serious between you two. Arms around you. Kissing you goodbye. Spill.'

After a moment's hesitation, Meghan announced bashfully, 'Apparently we're going camping.'

'Woo hoo,' Sally cried out, causing nearby diners to turn around and stare.

'Separate tents,' she clarified.

Sally wrinkled her nose. 'That's no fun.'

'Maybe not, but it makes sense at the moment,' Meghan pointed out.

'Well if Dusty's anything like with Alison, when he makes up his mind it'll happen fast and he'll sweep you off your feet.' Catching Meghan's frown of reflection, Sally said quickly, 'Sorry.'

Meghan shook her head. 'It's okay. I know I'm living in Alison's shadow,' she said quietly.

'Looks like Dusty's moving past that time in his life though.'

Although their chemistry was strong, Meghan and Dusty were being cautious, each for their own reasons, even though their hearts told them otherwise. She silently admitted that the attraction had grabbed her totally by surprise. So powerful from their first meeting, this was no passing fling and Meghan freaked out just thinking about hurdles ahead. For starters, one absent fiancé, plus she and Dusty lived in different countries half a world apart.

Sally leant over and gripped Meghan's arm. 'If it's true love, don't let anything come between you. Nothing. Do you understand me?'

'It's early days. I'd rather not talk about it anymore, okay?'

'Sure.'

The conversation moved on until they had drained their last cups of tea and Meghan checked her watch. 'I really should be heading back to school.'

'And I need to raid the IGA before heading back home.'

They hugged. 'I'll phone you after your camp-out.' She lowered her voice and winked. 'I expect to hear every detail, and don't leave out a thing.'

Meghan laughed but had her fingers crossed behind her back as she waved to Sally and they parted. Dusty didn't know everything about her and she wanted to tell him. She just needed the right moment. So it was with a huge sense of anticipation that Meghan welcomed his arrival within thirty minutes of school letting out the following Friday. He wanted to make camp by dark.

'Looking good enough to eat.' His shameless gaze lingered over her khaki shorts, white tank top and Akubra. 'But how am I supposed to find your mouth hidden under that big hat?' he drawled.

'You gave it to me,' she laughed as he scooped it off and he swept her into his arms.

The four-wheel drive was packed with camping gear and a portable freezer for food. As the sun sank over the low escarpment jutting out of the plains, they left the highway and headed into the bush, weaving through the scrubby mulga country along red dirt tracks until they found a clearing in a broad gully between two ridges.

On the drive out, Dusty explained that the area was one of the oldest landscapes in the world. She peered out at the huge red rocks and boulders of the granite outcrops forming a dramatic silhouette against the sky.

'The Wajarri people lived and travelled this country for thousands of years,' he said as they pulled up. 'Aboriginal culture was already sixty thousand years old when Europeans stumbled on it. You've seen their striking dot painting style and geometric designs in the artwork on the school buildings and in the town information centre by some of the local artists.'

'Yes, I bought one of them and one of Carrie's prints, too. As keepsakes of my time here.'

Dusty flashed her a troubled glance. 'I'll pitch the tents and you can gather wood for our campfire. But don't wander off too far.'

Meghan rambled, gathering dry twigs and small logs, returning to see one tent up and another unrolled from its kit. Meghan lingered, admiring a suntanned hatless Dusty bent to his task, muscles flexing as he worked. He turned and caught her staring.

She smiled and waved self-consciously. 'Just going for another load.'

When Meghan struggled back into camp with another armful of wood, Dusty had both tents pitched, the beginnings of a fire leaping into life and a portable barbeque ready to be placed over the coals when they burnt down. Two camp chairs were unfolded.

Meghan settled into one. 'This isn't camping. It's too comfortable.'

'Drink?' he offered.

'A beer would go down nicely.'

Dark fell over the mild evening and they watched the first stars appear. They listened to the silence staring into the fire, easy in each other's company. When the fire burnt down, they heated up the stew Meghan had made in the slow cooker while at school all day. She proudly produced a damper of unleavened bread dough wrapped in foil ready to be baked in the coals.

'We can take a walk up the hills tomorrow to get our bearings and a decent view of the countryside. And I can rig up a portable shower tomorrow. You'll feel like it after our hike.'

Later, his good-night kiss was long, slow and seductive.

Crawling into her lonely sleeping bag, Meghan wondered if she dared creep into the tent next door and surprise its occupant. Did he yearn for her too? While her mind buzzed with romantic thoughts of her camping companion, she must have fallen asleep; for next thing she knew, pale light showed through the canvas and she heard a carolling magpie outside.

She unzipped her tent to see Dusty with ruffled hair, unshaven and bare-chested, a pair of faded jeans sitting low on his hips. Meghan moaned. Hard not to streak over there and run her hands all over him.

After a breakfast of fried sausages, bacon and eggs on toast washed down with a huge mug of tea, they packed drinks, bread rolls, cheese and salami in an insulated backpack. By mid-morning they had secured their camp, locked the vehicle and were scrambling over rocky foothills of the red cliff escarpment jutting up from the plains.

'Keep an eye out for snakes,' Dusty warned and chuckled at Meghan's alarm. 'They'll hear you before you see them and probably disappear, but stay watchful.'

They took a break for a drink and a look back at their campsite below, then slowly pressed on to the top. In the shallow protected gully the air had been still, but as Dusty helped Meghan clamber over the last huge red boulders onto the top of the ridge, she was hit by the most wonderful refreshing breeze rushing up from below. She whipped off her hat and piled up her hair to cool off, looking out over the fading wildflower plains to the horizon.

Alongside, squinting out from beneath his black Akubra, Dusty handed her the water bottle. She gulped long draughts of the chill drink then handed it back.

In a surprise move, he bent toward her and licked beads of water still hovering on her lips, which turned into some serious kissing.

'We're supposed to be appreciating the view,' she murmured.

'I am.'

'Not objecting. Just saying.'

He chuckled and turned his gaze back to the scenery. 'What do you think of our breakaway country?'

'Beautiful. There's not much about the big west out here that I don't like.'

'Gets into your blood.'

Meghan patted her hat back onto her head. 'Lunch?'

Dusty unpacked the food and broke off chunks of bread while Meghan sliced cheese and salami with his pocket knife.

'Best meal I've ever eaten,' she declared later, washing it down with another swig of water.

Dusty laid back on the warm rock, pulled his hat over his face and dozed. It looked like a top idea so Meghan joined him. The warm air and gentle rustling of the wind flowing up from the gully soon made her drowsy. A while later she felt warm lips gently teasing her own.

With her eyes still shut, she said, 'Powerful grand being kissed awake.'

'We could make it a habit.'

Meghan's eyes flew open. 'Don't tempt me.'

'I'm trying to.'

'You're one bold fella, Dusty Nash. It's the strong, silent types we women have to watch.'

He smiled and pulled her up, watching her with dark glances while she snapped lots of photos. Meghan felt self-conscious to be so closely studied before they made their way back downhill again.

In the afternoon — so she didn't get lost, Dusty claimed — he tagged along behind her into the bush while she clicked madly again with her camera, capturing the landscape and wildflowers at their peak beauty. She regularly emailed photos back home to her parents and brother Kieran. Claire had gone quiet since her visit and she never heard from Dermot.

That night when the sinking sun made long golden fingers of light and shadow through the bush, Dusty stoked their campfire and they settled in for the night. As the moon rose and the fire crackled before them, Dusty stretched his boots toward the flames. Meghan glanced skyward to watch the first stars appear and the moon edge its way over the top of the surrounding ridges.

'The male moon is coming,' Dusty said.

'Male?' she queried wryly.

'Yes. Aboriginals believe the moon is male and the sun female.'

'You're letting on!'

'No. I learnt it from school growing up and from the Aboriginal workmen we've had on Sunday Plains over the years.'

Meghan shrugged. 'Every culture has its beliefs then. Irish history is full of folklore. The Druids and Celts believed in the power of magic. We heard tales of fairies playing pranks. Leprechauns hiding their gold at the end of a rainbow. I think they're all lovely and have a place.'

'I like the Aboriginal sun woman story the best. She lights a fire each morning.'

'The dawn?'

Dusty nodded. 'Then she lights her torch and travels across the sky creating daylight. As she descends to the western horizon, she puts out her torch and starts the long journey underground back to the morning camp in the east.'

Meghan's face beamed in the firelight. 'I like that.'

'Aborigines also believe in the continuing essence of a soul after death,' Dusty said. 'They believe only the moon escapes death and comes to life every month.'

'What a lovely belief.'

Meghan watched Dusty grow silent and reflective for a moment before he spoke again. 'After Alison died, on the night of the next full moon, I came out here and it felt like she was still with me.' He paused. 'I did it for a year.'

Meghan noted he spoke in the past tense. 'You don't come out anymore?' she queried softly.

He shook his head. 'I guess I'd gone through that initial phase of deep grief. And guilt,' he added quietly.

She snapped a glance at him and frowned. 'Guilt?' she whispered. 'Why?'

'I've never told anyone this.'

In her time here, Meghan had never seen this big man looking so vulnerable. In the firelight, his brows furrowed and he stared into the embers as he spoke.

'Everyone knew about the car accident of course, but not the reason behind it.'

Meghan had no idea what he was trying to say but waited until he continued.

'Alison was in Perth. Nothing unusual there. She was often down in the city.' He rubbed a hand across his forehead. 'I must have been over tired because when she phoned that day, I lost my cool. I supported her career one hundred percent, but I told her I missed her. Accused her of always putting her work before us and begged her to come back early. Her meeting was finished for the day but she planned to stay overnight and return next morning. Because I hassled her, she took an evening flight instead and was driving back out to Sunday Plains late at night.' He faltered. 'She must have been exhausted.'

Meghan moaned softly and sensed what might follow.

'I caused her accident.'

Meghan heard the blame in his troubled voice and said quickly, 'Bollocks. No one can possibly know that.' She ached to see this strong outback man brought down with such deep emotional pain. 'Jaysus, you've been to hell and back and you blame yourself? Sounds to me like it was just your normal accident. Could have happened to anyone, you know?'

'That's not all. We didn't know until they examined her in the hospital afterwards that she was also pregnant.' Meghan gasped. 'We'd been trying for two years.'

She groaned with regret for him, shuffled her chair closer and looped her arm through his, pressing herself closer in some measure of comfort. Dusty Nash had not only lost a wife that night but also a child as well.

'Life has regrets for us all.'

She thought of Dermot. In other circumstances, this idyllic night in the peace of the outback bush she might have told Dusty about him. Now it hardly seemed an appropriate moment to raise the subject when he had just confided in her and his emotions were open and raw.

'I'll never regret meeting you, Meghan,' Dusty murmured. 'You've brought laughter back into my life. You've given me hope and courage in the future.'

Her heart filled even more deeply with love for this man. 'I'm glad. You know I feel the same.'

For a while they both just sat in the aftermath of Dusty's revelation and stared into the glowing embers.

Eventually, he said, 'Thanks for listening. I feel so totally at ease with you.'

'Thank you for confiding in me. Not much reassurance maybe but sharing your thoughts like that might actually help. Do you think?'

'Hope so.'

Soon after, they rose and hugged. Their embrace turned to passionate kisses, releasing the emotions of the night.

'Go,' Dusty sighed, 'before I drag you into my sleeping bag and take advantage of you.'

'Promises, promises,' she teased.

He pushed a hand through his hair. 'Might take a walk. Clear my head.'

'Want company?'

He shook his head. 'Just need some space.'

'Sure.' She cupped his unshaven face in her hands. 'See you in my dreams.'

As she crawled into her sleeping bag alone for the second night, Meghan marvelled that Dusty had buried his guilt all this time.

*   *   *

Next morning, they broke camp and Dusty took her on a tour of the district, identifying points of interest, relating tales and history, and amazing Meghan with his depth of knowledge. He'd been born to this outback land as much as any native Aborigine. The day had grown overcast but the sun broke free from the heart of a cloud as they sped back toward town in the lengthening shadows of late afternoon.

Just as their relationship sparked into life and deepened, it was put on hold with shearing and early harvest. To her frustration, and with the weeks seeping away until she was due to leave, Meghan hardly saw Dusty at this busy time of the year. Occasionally, she begged a ride with Beth and travelled out to the homestead for a weekend. Dusty always seemed delighted to see her, but the two days flew and she left on Sundays disappointed they barely spent much time together.

As she waited in the utility one evening delivering a thermos of hot soup and salad rolls for the men working the night shift, Meghan watched the header munch its way across the plains and cut a wide path through the standing wheat.

When he reached her corner of the paddock again, Dusty pulled the giant monster of a header to a stop and climbed down the steps backwards to the ground. He pulled off his hat and wiped his damp forehead with the back of his arm even though he worked in an air-conditioned cabin. The evening heat settled over everything like a heavy blanket. Meaghan's heart filled at the sight of him

'You're a welcome vision.' He bent to kiss her. He smelled of dust and fuel and hard, honest labour. She handed him the cooler of food. 'Want to take a few rounds with me?' He nodded toward the mechanical beast behind them.

'Absolutely!'

She eagerly followed him across rows of prickly stubble straw. He climbed up first, then helped her up the steep ladder to sit on a small seat beside him. The cabin was bathed in light from the GPS and they moved off as Dusty lined up the machine to work through the paddock kilometres wide.

They stopped every half hour or so to offload the harvested grain into a waiting truck. Meghan was as excited as a child to be riding up so high beside the man she loved. Behind them, the huge header churned up clouds of dust and chaff. Sometimes the radio crackled into life with contact between Dusty and his team of men. But eventually the paddock was done and Dusty headed back to where she had parked the ute.

'Can you stay awake long enough to watch the sun come up?' he asked before she descended to the ground again.

'Sure. I'll set my alarm and grab a few hours sleep.'

She would steal any time she could with Dusty. School finished next week, her teaching post would be over and she was returning to Ireland. Her most crushing task had been booking her flight home, forcing her to accept her departure was real. Her fabulous time in Australia was racing to a close. Even the thought of being reunited with her family for Christmas didn't brighten her outlook. And then there was ending her engagement to Dermot.

11

When the alarm sounded to meet Dusty, Meghan scrambled from bed. Parting would be hard enough and she would miss him dearly. She groped her way through the homestead toward a kitchen light.

He was waiting and raised the can in his hand almost in apology. 'Just laying the dust with a beer.'

After the past exhausting weeks of harvest, he deserved a celebration. He had showered, his hair even more wavy when damp. He wore clean shorts and a checked shirt. Meghan felt inadequate in her cotton skirt and tank top, but his eyes roamed over her so tenderly she didn't care, and it seemed Dusty didn't either.

He tossed the ute keys in his hand and seemed anxious. 'Ready?'

She nodded, suspecting this dawn

rendezvous was an opportunity to say a private goodbye. She hoped she didn't break down and disgrace herself. He reached for her hand, snapped off the kitchen light and led her outdoors.

Although still dark, every star in the sky sparkled overhead and the faintest tinge of light in the east promised sunrise. The warm night settled over Meghan's bare skin like a soft shawl and she wound down the ute windows, letting the breeze whip her hair about. She didn't take particular notice where they drove, nor cared. When they stopped in the middle of a stubble paddock, they got out, he lowered the tailgate and they sat on it awaiting the sun.

'Should have brought a beer to crack open and celebrate the end of harvest.'

'I didn't realise how hard you worked in the heat.'

'Harvest can be tough for the womenfolk, too.'

'Sally and Beth love it.'

'They were born to it. It's not for everyone.'

'Well, I've loved every minute of my time in the outback,' she admitted softly.

'You were only here six months. Living here permanently would be different.'

'True. I feel like I've lived here longer, though. The community embraces everyone. Certainly made my arrival easier. And I'll never regret my decision to come out here.' How could she? She had met Dusty.

'Maybe we should have advertised for a teacher for a full year then?' He grinned.

'I still would have applied.'

Dusty's face grew serious. 'It's been a privilege to meet you, Meghan Dorney.'

'Thanks, but you can blame yourself. You were on the committee that chose me.'

'The decision was unanimous,' he drawled, narrowing his gaze toward the lightening horizon.

'Sun woman's nearly back to her morning camp,' she said absently.

'Meghan . . . '

'Mmm?'

'Do you reckon you could handle it out here? Permanently? The isolation,' he emphasised.

Meghan took a deep breath and crossed her fingers in the dark, breathless at the clues he was dropping. 'Positive.'

'It can be a tough life,' he warned.

'I hear the first six months are the worst,' she quipped.

He chuckled and sought her hand. 'Even an ordinary day feels special with you. After I lost Alison, I never thought I could love again, but it's happened so quickly and naturally with you.' He turned to her and said in a husky voice, 'I love you, Meghan Dorney.'

He slid off the tailgate, jumped down onto the ground and knelt down in the stubble. It took her so much by surprise that Meghan's mind scrambled before she realised what was happening.

Jaysus, his mind was even further along than hers. She panicked because as much as she wanted this, there was just one slight hitch. How could she promise herself to another man while still engaged? Her hands instinctively covered half her face in surprise. Her nose was tingling with emotion and she was well on the way to tears even before Dusty had opened his mouth to say a word.

She just wanted to push her fingers deep into his wavy hair and cup his face and bend down and kiss those gorgeous lips that looked like they were going to be hers for life. But she stopped her wild thoughts and focused on the moment. *Breathe. And don't miss a word.*

'Will you marry me, Meghan, and come and live with me on Sunday Plains?'

'Oh, my!' Meghan looked over his head. 'The colours!'

Dusty whipped around then stood up. Arms around each other, they shared the parade of colours that began with pale gold.

'She's lit the fire,' Meghan whispered.

Dusty kissed the top of her head and hugged her tighter. Quickly, as though impatient to show off, the sky turned to salmon then deepened to pink and rose, until the tip of an orange ball of sun peeped over the horizon, soon becoming an arc of flame and then a full circle.

'You haven't answered my question,' Dusty murmured.

Meghan turned into his arms. 'I didn't want us to miss the sunrise. That is why we came out here, isn't it?'

'Among other things.'

'And the answer's yes. I love you too, Dusty, and I'll marry you.'

'I don't have a ring. Yet.'

She paused. 'You know I have to go back to Ireland.'

Dusty nodded. 'Of course. It's Christmas. Your family will have missed you and want you back.'

It was time and there was no easy way to word it. 'There's something else

I need to do back home.'

Dusty raised his dark eyebrows and waited.

'There was someone else before I left.' In anguish, she watched Dusty's strong suntanned face cloud over warily. 'Technically he's still my . . . fiancé, but it's over and I'm going to break it off.'

'Fiancé!' Dusty pulled away and scowled. 'You're engaged?'

Bleakly, knowing how dreadful it sounded, Meghan nodded.

Dusty stiffened. He reached out across the distance between them and grabbed her left hand. 'You've never worn a ring.'

'I left it back home in Ireland. I only wore it for a matter of weeks before I realised it was a mistake.'

'Are you sure about me, then, if you still have unfinished business with this other man?'

'Of course.'

'I'm not a rebound for you?'

'Never. I've adored you since the first time I set eyes on you out on the road and you changed my tyre.' Meghan choked back a building fear.

'I feel like a fool. Taking another man's woman.' Dusty paced in the stubble, kicking up dust.

'Dusty, don't. It's not like that at all. That was the reason I came out here, to help me make that decision, but I knew in my heart even before I left that there wasn't anything holding us together anymore.' She looked down at her hands. 'That's why I left my ring back in Ireland. It didn't mean anything anymore.'

'What's his name?' Dusty asked quietly.

'Dermot O'Brien. He means nothing to me, Dusty, I promise.' She caught his desolate gaze. '*You're* my heart. *You* fill my life with meaning. I'm not his. I'm yours. If you still want me,' she pleaded in a small voice.

'Maybe it's best you go back and sort it out with your *fiancé*,' he stressed, 'then make a decision. You might change your mind.'

Meghan wildly shook her head. 'I won't.' She waited out the agonising silence that stretched between them. 'Don't you still want me?' she whispered, feeling cheap for asking.

'Best sort out your life first.'

'I just told you, it will be. It changes nothing between us.'

Dusty frowned. 'Why didn't you tell me sooner?' he accused.

'Because when I came out here and saw you it was like Dermot never existed. He became my past and I knew immediately that he no longer mattered in my life. My thoughts and feelings were only for you.'

Dusty pushed a hand through his hair and shook his head. Seeing his hurt and indecision when only moments before he had seemed so nervous and hopeful and then proposed, Meghan swallowed hard, fighting tears. 'We're still good, right?' Her heart would break if he said no.

He shrugged, sank his hands deep into his pockets and scuffed the dry red soil with his foot. 'It's been a shock to learn that you kept something secret that's so important.'

'I know,' she whispered. 'And I'm sorry for not telling you sooner, but I wanted to tell Dermot in person and that meant waiting until I went back.' A fateful ache wrapped itself around her heart and squeezed. Meghan winced. He didn't look at her, bewildered.

'I never loved Dermot, not like I love you.' Meghan fought for him, swallowing hard to stay in control and not become a blubbering mess. Dusty was shocked, saying nothing and, understandably, hurting. And it was her fault. Jaysus, what if he dumped her?

The drive back to the homestead was an ordeal. Desolate, Meghan folded her arms and stared out the window. She didn't know what she had expected but it wasn't this agonised silence. She felt cold waves of distrust radiate from him. She'd blown it. She would return to Ireland, call it off with Dermot, and then what was she supposed to do?

256

Contact Dusty? Leave it up to him? Forget him? Sunk low with misery, she stopped herself just short of bursting into tears.

As the ute pulled up before the homestead, Meghan scrambled out quickly and fled to the guest room. Ashamed of not being honest with Dusty sooner, she packed her bags and left, too afraid to face him. In her rear-view mirror as she drove away, Meghan saw him stroll out onto the front veranda, staring after her departing car.

Damn and blast, she cursed. She'd sure made a bags of it. On an impulse, she gritted her teeth for courage, planted her foot on the brake and backed up. The car whined and skidded in the gravel. She flung her door open, strode across the lawn, hair flying, and up the three wide steps to face him.

Hands on hips and breathing heavily, Meghan said to the scruffy gorgeous fella in front of her, 'Love is never walking away. It's standing your ground and sorting it out. I know I'm making a holy show of myself, but you've got to know. I love you. You're my fella. I don't want anyone else. I came clean and I've apologised, now it's up to you.'

Jaysus, grab me. Tell me to stay, she silently pleaded. *Tell me everything will be all right.*

But he just stood there rigid and Baltic. Big Dusty Nash didn't move a single one of his awesome muscles. His jaw clenched. 'Fair enough. I'll think on it.'

'Don't take too long. I'm in demand and not without my virtues. Which includes knowing how to change a tyre. Another man might snap me up just like that.' She clicked her fingers in his face.

Meghan thought she saw his lip twitch and waited. Still nothing. He wasn't planning to budge. Well, she would show this outback man she'd just as much backbone as him. So she turned on her heel and marched back to her car. She slammed the door, revved it up and spat up red dirt from its tyres as she hurtled away.

All the way back into Mallawa, Meghan muttered to herself, swaying between indignation and terror. She couldn't believe a man who claimed to love you would let you go. If she'd learned one thing from her failed relationship with Dermot and six months in Australia, it was that two people had to feel the same about each other. Half-hearted didn't work. She'd been the biggest fool to even consider Dermot's proposal a year ago. Now she'd been offered the same chance with the love of her life and she'd thrown it away.

★　★　★

The town farewell in the pub was a nightmare. Meghan plastered a fake smile on her face until her cheeks ached, but any tears she shed were real as she said goodbye to so many friends. Carrie and Noreen. Barbara and all her fellow teachers and kids from school, both brown faces and white. She loved them all. By the end of the night, and Meghan hoped it wasn't the result of too many Australian beers, she had an open invitation to come back and stay with almost everyone in town.

Beth grasped both her hands in her own and gently smiled. 'We shall miss you, dear. I thought . . . '

'Future's never certain,' Meghan said quickly.

Sally drew her aside later, her face shining. 'We'll be away for a week in Perth soon. For IVF treatment,' she said and let her announcement sink in before she added, 'We're trying for another baby.'

Meghan gasped, grabbed her hands and pulled her into a teary hug. 'Oh, I wish you all the luck in the world. I should have brought a four-leaf clover with me, shouldn't I?' *For more reasons than one, Meghan* thought miserably. 'What about Ollie?'

'He'll stay with Mum.'

'Keep in touch.'

'What about my big brother then?' Sally leaned close and whispered.

'We're still good friends.'

Sally scowled at Meghan's half-hearted assurance. Then Phil and Ollie scooped her into two equally vigorous hugs, almost her undoing.

Dusty was there, of course. Hovering. He'd been on the original selection committee, so it would hardly look right if he'd not turned up. He circulated, glared at Meghan but smiled at everyone else. When the night wound up, he crossed the room purposely toward her and her heart lifted. Then he shook her hand. *He shook her hand.* Like a stranger. In public.

She had nothing to lose so she leant forward and planted a firm warm kiss on his cheek. 'Take care.'

He barely flinched. Somehow she managed not to become Niagara Falls and walked away.

Next day, as Meghan drove west back to Geraldton to catch the first leg of her flight home and only when she was finally alone, she let the hot hurtful tears fall. She sobbed and muttered with anger and regret. What if Dusty didn't want her back? She should have told him sooner.

It took a moment before she heard the car thumping. She must have hit or run over something on the road but being upset, she hadn't noticed. Unwelcome grisly images flashed into her mind of a dead animal caught up beneath the car.

She slowed down and pulled over onto the verge. Preparing herself for some grim discovery, Meghan prowled around her car and let out a gasp of amazement. No injured wildlife, but another flat tyre! What were the odds? Seeing the irony, Meghan laughed through her tears and cursed as she set about changing it. How ironic.

She alternately slept and cried at thirty thousand feet all the way home. She had to face Dermot, but did she have the courage to beg Dusty to take her back? Could she face the humiliation of rejection?

★ ★ ★

Her Irish reunion with family and friends, including a reserved Claire, barely took her mind off her aching loss for Dusty. The grey sky and cold rain hit her with surprise. When had Ireland become so dismal? she wondered.

Being almost Christmas, Dorney's pub accommodation was fully booked, but Aileen and David had kept one of the lovely but small attic bedrooms free for their daughter until she decided where she would live. Not with Dermot in his fancy apartment anymore, that was for sure. Gossip at the bar was that Claire and Dermot O'Brien were an item anyway. Meghan wished she could brag that she had a man of her own to stop the pitying glances sent her way.

Within twenty-four hours of her return, Meghan trudged uphill in the rain to Dermot's place feeling chilled to the bone. She had sent him a text and arranged to meet when he was briefly free. She entered his apartment early, letting herself in with her key and a small box tucked into her coat pocket. His place was all black and steel and glass. Once, she had thought this so posh.

When Dermot arrived, they regarded each other like distant friends. Meghan considered the designer suit and matching tie, the neat haircut and polished appearance that had once sent her heart into a flutter. Impossible not to compare him with a rugged tanned Aussie bloke whose smile weakened her knees and to whom she had *really* lost her heart.

'You're looking well,' he said.

'You, too.' She fished for the box in her pocket and handed it to him. 'It was beautiful but too grand for me. Claire will love it, though. She won't mind if it's second-hand.' As an afterthought, she added, 'Treat her right, Dermot, or you'll answer to me.'

Dermot would never stoop so low as to look guilty, but he nodded and held out his hand. Meghan shook it. Seemed like all the men in her life were trickling like winter rain through her fingers lately. Two down, none to go.

She returned to work in the pub, pulling beers and serving grub until the New Year when she would resume teaching at the local school again. On Christmas Day, a loud and happy Dorney family shut the stained-glass pub doors and gathered around a roaring fire against the freezing cold and pouring rain outside. Sitting on the plush red carpet, Conor and Abby tore the paper off their presents, including the cuddly soft koalas Aunt Meghan had brought them back from Australia.

Feeling like an outsider looking in on them all eating, drinking, smiling and happy, Meghan sighed and glanced out the window. The sun would be shining on Sunday Plains.

★ ★ ★

On the same day in Australia, it was hot. At Sunday Plains homestead, the Nash and Barnes families similarly gathered to celebrate Christmas. Sally and Phil were back from Perth, buoyed and hopeful that their fertility treatment would succeed. Dusty and Sally's older sister, Sophie, had flown west from her property in South Australia, a rare and special visit.

'A bunch of geologists are coming out to Casuarina Downs for research. Some university guy with 'Doctor' in front of his name,' Sophie announced.

Later, Sally noticed Dusty saunter alone outside onto the patio and followed. A flaming sunset streaked the sky before another warm humid night settled around them.

'You're missing her.'

'Not sure she's right for out here.' Sally raised her eyebrows in question. 'She had to return to Ireland anyway. Her work visa's up. Besides, we had . . . words before she left. Not sure I'm welcome.'

Sally nudged her shoulder against him. 'Liar. I've never known you to back away from anything. I hope you've bought a plane ticket.'

He chuckled. 'Don't nag. Just letting her sweat a little.'

'Dusty Nash!' Sally said, horrified. 'You devil. How could you? She'll be a wreck.'

★ ★ ★

Meghan wasn't particularly keeping track of the days, but it was somewhere between Christmas and New Year on a quiet morning before opening. Aileen was upstairs doing the books and David was down in the cellar. She was washing glasses with her back turned to the pub door when the hairs all over her body bristled. She shivered, and it wasn't from the cold gusting in the doorway.

She frowned, spun around and dropped the glass. He'd come for her. Jaysus, he was worth the wait.

267

He swaggered up to the bar in a long wool-lined coat, rain dripping from the wide brim of his Akubra. 'Have you ditched the other man?'

Meghan took a deep breath and nodded. 'First thing. Being free now, I'm getting offers daily, so if you're still interested you'd best be showing your hand or stand in line. Are you on holidays then?'

'Yep.'

'Where?'

'Just here.'

'Nowhere else?'

'Nowhere else has quite the same . . . attractions.' He shrugged. 'Except maybe Sunday Plains.'

'Are you sure you didn't get lost now?'

'A heart always finds its way home,' he murmured.

'That a fact. And whose heart would you be trying to find then?'

'You're a clever woman. You'll guess.'

'Fair play to you, Dusty Nash. I'm forgiven then?' she asked coyly.

'You scared the hell out of me. I thought I had competition.'

'So, you're here now. Am I worth it?'

'I'd walk over hot coals to get to you, Meghan Dorney,' he drawled. 'Fortunately, it was just a very long plane ride.' He pulled a wry grin.

His direct gaze settled on her and she squirmed with excitement. This man was proving a slow burner for sure. The future was looking brighter by the second.

'You could have told me all this in Australia and saved yourself a heap of time, you know that, don't you?'

'You threw a spanner into the works. I wanted you to be sure.'

'Don't give me your smooth talking swagger, Dusty Nash. Thinking you look so hot in your tight dusty jeans and your big hat pulled down so low and mysterious a girl can't even see your eyes.'

'Then she'd be wise to come a little closer.'

'You think you're such a turn-on.'

'A fella can hope.'

Meghan's voice lowered and she swaggered around from behind the bar. 'And he can also be opening his mouth to say what he really means.' She uncrossed her arms and prowled toward him with purpose, swinging her sassy Irish hips. 'Spit it out, cowboy. You're making a bags of it,' she teased.

They both knew why he'd come. For her. She just needed to hear him say it.

Bowled over by her confidence on home territory — a situation he aimed to change — and with his body jet-lagged from too much flying, Dusty let Meghan do all the work and waited until she was only an arm's length away and within easy reach. He could see the gleam in her eye and already tasted the soft lips he was about to claim. He darted out a strong arm and wrapped it around her waist, dragging her against him.

Gasping and laughing, she said, 'So, actions speak louder than words, then? I do like a man who knows his mind.'

'And his woman.'

'Well, as a teacher, I have to tell you I consider you a slow learner.'

Meghan scooped off his big well-worn Akubra, the one she loved so much and that was as much a part of him as the air he breathed, and tossed it aside onto the floor. She pushed her hands up into that thick mass of familiar sandy hair and wrapped one leg seductively and possessively around his. Their mouths met hungrily, tongues entwined, and the world was lost. Dusty ran his hands all over her body.

'Jaysus Christ, Meggie Dorney, the man's eatin' ye. If you young ones can't be decent in public, take it private,' an elderly man muttered from the doorway.

'Oh, for Christ's sake, Lenny Doyle,' Meghan broke off in disgust, breathing rapidly, 'we're not open for at least another hour and you'd be knowing it.'

'I allus take me seat by the door. I can wait.'

'Please yourself.' Meghan shrugged. 'As long as you don't mind a floor show while you're waiting.' She turned back to Dusty. 'Do you think you could manage that, farmer Nash?'

He couldn't reply because he was laughing and shaking his head.

'I'm hopin' he'll do more than nibble around the edges, Lenny,' Meghan growled. 'So you'd best make yourself scarce. Wouldn't want you taking a turn at your age.'

'I'm perfect fit and able. Just ask my Moira. But if it's going to be turnin' dirty in here . . . ' he muttered and shuffled out again.

'Lock the door, Lenny,' Meghan cried out urgently.

★ ★ ★

Outside the whitewashed Dorney's pub, two old men, caps on their heads and huddled inside their coats, sat by the door on a wooden bench seat. Smoking quietly, they half turned at the sound of crashing coming from inside.

'Not much talkin' goin' on in there.'

'With a pair of legs like those on Meggie Dorney you'd not be wastin' yer breath talking, Lenny.'

His drinking mate leaned closer. 'Should we take a peek in the winder, do you think? Make sure she's all right?'

'Our Meggie can take care of a big man like that. He'll look after her, I reckon. Hope they're not too long. Me thirst's growin'.' He checked his pocket watch. 'Only another ten or fifteen minutes till openin' anyway.'

'Place'll be a mess when they finally open. Might have trouble gettin' to the bar.'

'Aye, that'd be a problem for sure.'

'You've never gone up to the bar in yer whole life. Aileen always serves you and your table.'

'She has her eye on me, that woman.'

'A lass of her age? Not unless she's blind.' He paused. 'Do you hear that?'

Lenny cupped a hand to his ear. 'Can't hear a thing.'

'That's right. Commotion's stopped inside.'

'Ye eejit, you shouldna locked the door. We coulda gone inside now and set by the fire.'

Lenny snorted. 'Who said I locked it?'

The two old men looked at each other and shared a wily grin.

* * *

Six months later, an Irish-Australian wedding was held on Sunday Plains in outback Western Australia. The bride carried a real horseshoe for good luck, turned up so the luck didn't run out, but she doubted it would any time soon. Both the circlet in her hair and her bouquet were wildflowers.

Tables were set up outside on the lawns among the trees, decorated with fairy lights and butterflies. Lanterns placed throughout the garden gave off a soft warm glow, adding to the romantic atmosphere of the gloriously mild autumn night. A band set up and played both Irish and Australian music from the back of a truck parked in the yard.

For the second time in six months, Dusty's sister Sophie flew over again from her sheep station property Casuarina Downs in South Australia.

All of Meghan's family had arrived from Ireland. Her parents, David and Aileen, brother Kieran and his wife Fiona with their children, Conor and Abby. They planned on travelling around Australia together in a mobile home after the wedding.

A glowing Sally revealed she was pregnant, and was already starting to show a rounded tummy which everyone fondly referred to as 'the bump'.

Claire graciously attended as bridesmaid, a familiar large diamond ring on her left hand. Dermot wasn't invited. 'It's an adventure visiting you, Meggie, for sure, but I'd not want to be living out here.'

After the ceremony, the guests drank Black Velvets and danced till dawn.

Before the newlyweds left for an extended

honeymoon on the Coral Coast in a luxury secluded beach house, they visited the cemetery so Meghan could leave her wedding bouquet on Alison's grave.

'She'll always be a part of our lives and never forgotten.' She smiled up at her rugged suntanned husband.

'My sentiments exactly.'

She stood on tiptoe and kissed him. Life was about moments, Meghan knew, and released a long, happy sigh. Today was surely one of them.

THE END

We do hope that you have enjoyed reading this large print book.

Did you know that all of our titles are available for purchase?

We publish a wide range of high quality large print books including:
Romances, Mysteries, Classics
General Fiction
Non Fiction and Westerns

Special interest titles available in large print are:
The Little Oxford Dictionary
Music Book, Song Book
Hymn Book, Service Book

Also available from us courtesy of Oxford University Press:
Young Readers' Dictionary
(large print edition)
Young Readers' Thesaurus
(large print edition)

For further information or a free brochure, please contact us at:
Ulverscroft Large Print Books Ltd.,
The Green, Bradgate Road, Anstey,
Leicester, LE7 7FU, England.
Tel: (00 44) **0116 236 4325**
Fax: (00 44) **0116 234 0205**

Other titles in the
Linford Romance Library:

ROMANCE IN THE AIR

Pat Posner

After ending a relationship she discovered was based on lies, Annie Layton has sworn off men. When her employers, Edmunds' Airways, tell her they're expanding, she eagerly agrees to help set up the sister company. Moving up north will get her away from her ex — and the Air Ministry official who's been playing havoc with her emotions. But Annie hadn't known exactly who she'd be working with ... Will she find herself pitched headlong into further heartache?

ANGELA'S RETURN HOME

Margaret Mounsdon

It has been years since schoolteacher Angela Banks last saw Russ Stretton, but she remembers him only too well. She'd had a massive crush on him as a teenager, and now he was back in her life. But he's carrying considerable emotional baggage, including a five-year-old son, Mikey — not to mention a sophisticated French ex-wife, who seems intent on winning him back at all costs . . .

THE LOVING HEART

Christina Green

Lily Ross becomes nursemaid to young Mary, whose widowed father runs Frobisher's Emporium in their seaside village in Devon. She loves her job caring for Mary, a good-natured and spirited child. Although Matt, her fisherman friend, worries her with his insistent love that she cannot return, other things fill her life: Mary and her adventures, the strange flower lady — and her growing feelings for her employer, Mr Daniel. But as his nursemaid she must keep her feelings to herself, or risk losing her position . . .

THE FATAL FLAW

Anne Hewland

When a young woman wakes with no memory of her identity, she is told by Charles Buckler that he has rescued her from a vicious attack during her journey to Ridgeworth to become the intended bride of his distant cousin, Sir Ashton Buckler. An impostor has taken her place, however, and she must resume her rightful position. Who can Elinor believe? Is Charles all he seems? What happened to Sir Ashton's first wife — and why does someone at Ridgeworth resent her presence?

AFTER ALL THESE YEARS

Natalie Kleinman

When Guy Ffoulkes walks into Honeysuckle Bunting's teashop after fourteen years, her world is turned upside-down. Guy was her bother Basil's best friend; she was Basil's scruffy younger sister. For Honey, though, there had always been more. Guy left Rills Ford at eighteen to go to university, kissing the top of Honey's head in a brotherly fashion. She was heartbroken . . . Now Guy has returned from Australia, a rich and successful architect — and when Honey discovers what his first local project will be, she is horrified . . .